SG    X

# Trouble in Tucson

Hasty Jones was an ordinary guy, scratching a living from the harsh land that was southern Arizona. But he had one flaw: a temper. They didn't call him Hasty for nothing.

And it was that temper that put him into Yuma Pen for killing a man. When he finally emerged he was confident that he had learned his lesson, that he could hold his explosive nature in check and that he could put his past behind him.

But that was not the way it was to be. Danger would stalk his every step.

# Trouble in Tucson

Sean Kennedy

**A Black Horse Western**

ROBERT HALE · LONDON

© Sean Kennedy 2005
First published in Great Britain 2005


ISBN 0 7090 7630 4

Robert Hale Limited
Clerkenwell House
Clerkenwell Green
London EC1R 0HT


The right of Sean Kennedy to be identified as
author of this work has been asserted by him
in accordance with the Copyright, Designs and
Patents Act 1988.

Typeset by
Derek Doyle & Associates, Liverpool.
Printed and bound in Great Britain by
Antony Rowe Limited, Wiltshire

*Für Helga und Karl*

# PROLOGUE

*Arizona Territory, somewhere near the border*

'The bozo's looking for trouble and he's gonna cause us trouble. One way or another I want him out of the way.'

'Name the time and place.'

'Have you ever ridden long distance over unknown terrain?'

'Yeah.'

'It is pointed out that in such circumstances it is a wise thing to halt now and again, to stretch one's legs, check the horse and enquire as to the conditions of the trail; to consider one's bearings. Thus fatigue of horse and rider is lessened and the risk of losing one's way is minimized.'

The listener's eyes were blank as the brain behind them searched for meaning in the words.

'The implication,' the other sighed, 'is that there

are times when one should stay one's hand for a spell. Opportunities have a habit of making themselves available.'

# ONE

A neat runabout with lazy-back top rolled across the saguaro-studded flat past Fort Lowell and into Tucson. At the reins Louise Hammersley threaded the vehicle through the traffic of the Calle Real and came to a halt at the side of one of the town's many plazas. After disembarking, she negotiated a price with a bright-eyed Mexican boy to look after the rig, and moved onto the sidewalk with her companion, Charlotte Jones.

They were in town to buy trappings for the evening's shindig at the Triple C. The owner, Old Ben Matthews, was the cattle king of the Santa Cruz and every year he organized a barbecue and dance for his neighbours. For most of the modestly living farmers it was the highlight of their social calendar.

Charlotte did not care much for Louise, a buxom, bouncy woman with a friendly outward demeanour but with a reputation as a scandal-monger and an inveterate nag of her husband. So, in normal circumstances, Charlotte would not have chosen her company. But, always relishing a chance to show off her neat buggy and handsome trotter, the woman had suggested a joint shopping spree in town. Charlotte would like to have used some excuse to decline; however, as the offer was made in company all of whom knew she needed a dress for the occasion, she had found it difficult to refuse.

They toured the likely stores and, after much fussy deliberation, made their purchases, Louise opting for a flashy mutton-sleeved bombazine dress while Charlotte went for a simple gingham frock.

When they were outside with their packages, Louise fanned her face. 'After that we need a rest and some refreshment,' she said. 'I know just the place. It's not only cool but they serve an excellent *cafecito*.'

They moved further down the Calle Real and stepped into The Pavilion Café. They passed through the dining-room to the back and were guided to seats in the shaded patio.

Charlotte was covered in a heavy shawl. Although the afternoon heat was sweltering, the sky had been overcast earlier in the day prompting her to bring it. She had not needed it but, loath to leave it in the buggy, she had no recourse but to wear it. Before sitting she draped the encumbrance over the back of her seat.

While they were waiting for their drinks she looked around, noting that the clothing of the other

10

patrons reflected the expensiveness of the place.

'I always come here,' Louise said sniffily. 'You could dine here for a week and not hear two words of Mex. They have such a decent class of customer.' Then she leaned forward and whispered, 'Except for him.'

Her eyes were flicking in the direction of a lone figure at a far table. A metal shield gleamed in his lapel but his dapper clothes didn't accord with the normal work-a-day garb that one might expect of a lawman.

'Sheriff Syson,' Louise continued in hushed tones after their drinks had been served. 'Has trouble keeping his pants on when he's alone with a lady. Thinks he's God's gift to the fair sex. Mind, one does have to admit he's handsome.'

Charlotte said nothing. She had had her own experiences with him. Several times the man had fawned over her during visits to town. On one occasion her husband Fred had overheard his oily overtures and, in his down-to-earth way, had threatened to rework the man's face so he would lose his attraction to women. It had taken all Charlotte's powers of persuasion to stop him carrying out his threat there and then on the Tucson boardwalk.

'Left his calling card, they say,' Louise carried on. 'There's talk of more than one woman's child in the territory who doesn't have her husband's looks.'

But she stopped her whispering when he looked their way.

11

'Howdy, ladies,' he greeted in a deep, resonant voice. They nodded in decorous acknowledgement.

'Are you good ladies going to the Cruz social this evening?' he went on.

'Yes, indeed,' Louise said.

'I'm afraid I won't have the pleasure of your company,' he said. 'This is the first year I've missed it. My deputy's got some family business to attend to so I have to stay in town on duty. Very regrettable, but there it is.'

It was a heartfelt regret. To him the merrymaking into the night was a golden opportunity to pursue his lusts.

He stood up and walked towards them, hat in one hand, cup and saucer in the other. Close up he was even more handsome, save a left cheekbone ridged with parallel rows of scars like he'd been clawed by some wild animal – or some wild woman.

'May I join you, ladies?'

'By all means you may sit at this table,' Louise said, 'but I'm afraid we're planning to leave now.'

'Oh, I'm sorry to hear that,' he said. Charlotte took her cue from Louise and rose.

'Allow me,' he said, taking the shawl from the chair. He bent near her ear as he put it in place over her shoulders. His voice was hardly audible. 'If ever you can't get satisfaction between the sheets from that dirt farmer husband of yours, my dear, you know where to come.'

'Sheriff Syson,' Charlotte snapped, wrenching

away from him, 'you are out of order. I must ask you not to speak to me again. Come, Louise.'

'Well, I never,' Louise said when they were outside. The lawman had kept his voice low, intending his words to be heard only by one pair of ears. But he hadn't reckoned on those of Mrs Hammersley. Her flaps could pick up the sound of a mouse's paws at a hundred paces.

'Whatever you do,' Charlotte said as they bustled back towards their buggy, 'don't tell anybody. Especially my Fred. You know what he's like. They don't call him Hasty for nothing.'

The Jones family set out in their wagon while it was still light. Charlotte was in her new gingham dress while Hasty and their son were in their Sunday-go-to-meeting clothes. Normally little Jimmy sat in the back, but tonight was special so he was positioned in between his parents even though there was barely room for the three of them on the front seat.

As they journeyed, the sun gradually disappeared behind the Santa Rita Mountains and the sound of the hummingbirds of the day was replaced by the gentle swishing of bats. A mile before they reached their destination, they could see the main complex of the Cruz Cattle Company glowing its welcome in the dark.

Hasty was familiar with the layout of the place. Born a Texan, he had run into Ben Matthews and his men when they were buying cattle in Texas and Ben had invited him to join the crew getting the beef back to Arizona. Back at the Cruz the old man could see the youngster was a willing worker and offered him a permanent job with the outfit. Thus it was that his first long-term job had been working for the Cruz Cattle Company and it was his years there that had provided the wherewithal for getting married. In fact it had been at one of Ben Matthews' annual barbecues that he had first met Charlotte. Careful with his dollars and not prone to drinking or gambling, unlike many of his fellow workers in the outfit, Hasty had eventually gathered enough to buy a quarter-section upon which he had set up home with his new bride.

He nosed the wagon alongside others parked near the festivities. The threesome stepped down and made their way towards the main building, passing Mexican labourers turning a variety of stock – pig, lamb and a steer – on spits over roaring fires. Here and there the couple exchanged felicitations with familiar faces. An accordionist, accompanied by a fiddler with his instrument propped against his lower ribs in the old-fashioned way, played on one side of the courtyard while tables festooned with platters of food were set out on the other.

'I must say,' Hasty said, 'you can always rely on the old man to splash out. I ain't seen so much grub together in one place since—'

'—since last year's shindig,' his wife interjected.

Suddenly Jimmy spotted some of his school-

14

friends. 'Can I go and play, Ma?'

'In a moment, Son,' Hasty said. 'We gotta be polite and pay our respects to the old feller first.'

He conducted his family across the huge courtyard, bathed in the multi-coloured light from Chinese lanterns strung between the trees.

The *casa principal* was a substantial building with a long gallery running the length of the frontage and Ben Matthews was seated in a wheelchair surveying the festivities. 'Thank you for inviting us, Mr Matthews,' Hasty said as they mounted the steps.

'Ha, Hasty,' the old man said. 'Good to see you again.'

'You remember my wife Charlotte.'

'Of course. Pleased you could come, ma'am.' The oldster patted the Indian-patterned blanket covering his legs. 'My only regret is I am unable to take advantage of your presence to dance with such a beautiful guest.'

'I regret that too, sir,' she said.

The *patron* turned his attention to Jimmy. 'And it's good to see your little boy, too. How old is he now?'

'Five,' Hasty replied, adding, 'but he likes to say pushing six.'

The old man chuckled. 'Believe me, son, when you get older you'll start counting the other way. Anyways, you're growing into a fine man. Just like your pa. One of the best hands I ever had on the payroll.'

He looked back at Hasty. 'And how you making out?'

'Getting by, sir.'

'You've got what it takes to make a go of it but remember what I've told you: if ever you run into bad times breaking the earth out there, there's always a job for you back here.' He gestured towards the gaiety. 'Meantimes, eat, drink, dance, and enjoy yourselves.'

Jimmy skipped off to join his pals while his parents took glasses of punch and mixed with other guests. After a few drinks they chanced a few steps dancing in the throng on the adobe paving of the courtyard.

Then they helped themselves to food and more drinks. With the maturing of the evening, the numbers under the sparkling brightness of the lanterns depleted as young couples lost themselves in solitary walks in the darkness.

A youthful puncher, eager to make display before the young ladies, took to the floor by himself and executed some complicated cavorting amidst much loud thumping and laughter.

Hasty guided his wife away, shaking his head. 'Younkers today. Ain't they a hell of a lot noisier than we were?'

'No, they ain't any noisier. That's just a sign you're getting older, you bozo.'

Hasty grinned as he recognized the growl, and turned. 'Mel Adams, well I'll be.'

Mel Adams was one of the Triple C punchers, an old working comrade and close friend of Hasty's.

Hasty grabbed his hand. 'How you doing, pal?' He

16

stepped back and assessed the man, face gleaming, hair slicked down. 'Jeez, I ain't seen you so well-scrubbed since you was best man at our wedding.'

Mel ignored the comment and took Charley's hand. 'How you doing, ma'am?'

And thus the evening proceeded. A chance to make merry and meet old friends. As on previous times, an enjoyable happy occasion. That is until they came across Louise Hammersley and her husband.

The chatter was of a casual nature and of no consequence – until Louise said, 'We were most affronted in town today.'

Charlotte could see what was coming and tried to quiet the woman with a concentrated stare and shake of her head. Maybe it was too dark or the message too subtle to see, but Louise continued. 'That ill-mannered sheriff of ours. Do you know what he said to Charlotte when we were minding our own business taking refreshment in the Pavilion Café?'

'No, please, Louise,' Charlotte pleaded.

'What?' Hasty demanded.

The woman leant forward in conspiratorial fashion. 'The man said, "If ever you can't get satisfaction between the sheets from that dirt farmer husband of yours, you know where to come". My, what a thing to say. Would you believe it?'

Hasty not only believed it – but exploded. 'That critter! The greasy sidewinder!' He spluttered and fumed incoherently. Then: 'He's gone too far this time. It's about time I sorted out that varmint's hash once and for all.' And with that he stormed across the courtyard, oblivious to the dancers and music.

Mounting the gallery steps he presented himself before Mr Matthews. 'Sir, something's cropped up and I need to get to town at once. Can I borrow a horse?'

'I hope it's not something serious. But of course you may take a horse. You know where the stable is. Take the pinto. He's quite docile with unfamiliar riders.'

Hasty loped through the darkness to the stable. By the time he had unfastened the door and was inside the building, Charlotte was behind him. 'No, Hasty. It's not important.'

Without speaking, he lit a lantern and looked along the stalls till he had identified the pinto.

'Louise shouldn't have said anything,' she repeated in distraught fashion as she watched him saddling up. 'You know what a tittle-tattle she is.'

He heaved a saddle off the stand, still without speaking. She grabbed his arm but he wrenched away and placed the saddle on the pinto.

'You know he doesn't mean anything to me,' she cried as he cinched up. 'This is madness.'

But he was deaf to all her words; mute, too, mounting up without speaking and slapping the horse's flank to plunge into the darkness.

He thundered along the old wagon road at a mile-eating pace. In his frame of mind he could have lost the way; worse, given the speed he was pushing the

18

horse, the animal could have mis-footed in the darkness; but he knew every rut of the trail, keeping the horse to the side, away from the two deep grooves worn into the packed earth.

Moreover, for a great deal of the journey the clouds kept away from the three-quarter moon, and he made Tuscon without mishap. He curved into the Calle Real and pulled his horse to a sudden, sliding stop outside the law office, oblivious to the alkali dust whirling past him.

The place was in darkness. He grunted in frustration and looked up and down the street. With many folks out at the Cruz shindig, the town was virtually deserted and most of the drinking parlours had closed early.

Then he noticed a glimmer a few blocks on. He heavy-footed down the street disdaining the boardwalk. The light was coming from the San Pedro saloon.

He bust through the swing doors. And there in all his smart-suited finery, standing at the bar, was Sheriff Syson.

'You snake-in-the-grass lecher,' Hasty hissed. 'You been messing with my woman.'

The sheriff turned, sucked on his teeth and gave him a stare till he recognized him.

'She's a might handsome woman, Jones, no mistake, but I don't mess with another man's woman.'

'Hell, you're a liar too. But the time for talking's

over.' And with that Hasty launched himself forward, jabbing his fist hard into the man's face. His short lifetime cowpunching and on farms had been enough to pack the young man's body with brawn and the sheriff staggered back under the impact. The lawman started to go down, but held himself against the bar. Pulling himself erect he shook his head and looked at the blood on the back of the hand that he had wiped across his mouth. He stepped back and drew his gun but Hasty was on him again, wrenching the weapon from his hand and fisting him in the jaw.

In the second that Hasty was throwing aside the gun, the sheriff swung a fist into his stomach and the young man lurched back with a grunt, doubling up, momentarily winded.

'You know the rules, gentlemen,' the bartender said in bored, routine tones during the lull. 'You do your scrapping outside.'

The sheriff looked at the speaker for a second, then took advantage of the pause to circle his adversary and make for the door, not to continue the issue outside as recommended, but simply to make good his escape.

He had just cleared the batwings when Hasty bust through after him, the impetus of his weight throwing the sheriff to the boards.

'Good enough time for me to close up,' the bartender said, yawning and glancing up at the clock. He'd seen scraps before, this was no different; and his bed took priority. He crossed the room and began locking the doors, virtually oblivious to the sound of the ruckus on the other side.

Outside, the two men were back on their feet, swinging wildly at each other in the darkness. In the stillness of the night all that could be heard was the scuffle of their feet on the boards and the panting and gasping with the exertion. They grappled for a spell until Hasty got his right hand clear and, using every pound in his body, swung a haymaker into the other's man's face. The sheriff reeled backwards and fell to the boards, his head clunking against a stanchion. Hasty looked down at him. There was a strange, choking sound in the man's throat, blood trickled from his nostrils and his head lolled to one side. He was out for the count. In that case, Hasty thought, enough was enough.

Still maintaining his vigil on the figure he stepped back, sucking in air. But in the darkness he didn't realize how close he was to the edge of the boardwalk and his right foot suddenly stepped on thin air. He keeled over backwards into the street, his head smashing against the bar of the hitchrail on the way down.

It was a solid connection, enough to put him out.

He didn't know how long he was unconscious. All he knew was – hands shaking him to his senses; he opened his eyes to see a crowd around him. Between their legs he could see the figure of his opponent still sprawled out. But with the saloon door now open again and light cascading on to the boardwalk he could now see there was an unnatural, awkward angle to the man's head against the stanchion. And the man was in the same position as he last remembered him.

Was the sheriff still knocked out?

His question was answered seconds later.

'He's killed the sheriff!' someone shouted 'Hasty Jones has killed Sheriff Syson!'

# TWO

By mid-morning there was a noisy crowd outside the law office. Ted Murray, Syson's deputy who had been quickly sworn in as acting sheriff, looked out of the window and chewed agitatedly on his tobacco. It was difficult to say why the mob was so vociferous. Syson had not been a popular sheriff. But he had kin and some friends. Maybe they were at the heart of it. Or maybe the town just didn't cotton to somebody killing their elected sheriff – especially somebody who was not one of them. No matter how long Hasty Jones had lived and worked in their Arizona he was still a Texan.

Murray saw somebody struggling to get through the crowd. It was the mayor.

'They're looking a bit ugly,' the sheriff observed when the official finally made it through the door. 'I don't know how long I can hold them off. I need a deputy.'

'I can fix that,' the mayor said. 'There's young

Drew Clayton for a start. He's a capable guy and looking for a job.' But before he could say anything else, a stone came through a window, sprinkling him with glass shards. He jumped back apprehensively. 'But I don't think just getting you a deputy will be enough. We're angling for Arizona to become a state, and the Justice Department has got us under the magnifying glass. We've got to show them we can handle our own law and order.'

He listened to the racket coming through the broken window. 'And the last thing we want is a lynching.' He thought on it. 'As soon as I've sworn in a deputy, I'll send him to Fort Lowell. I'll get him to explain the situation to them and request they keep Jones in the guardhouse there. That should be adequate protection until US marshals arrive.'

News was some time getting to Hasty's wife out in the homestead and it was a very distraught Charlotte who eventually came to visit him in his cell.

Sobs racked her body as she wrapped her arms round him. 'What's going to happen to you?'

He pulled her head close, his fingers entwining her hair. 'Don't know, Charley. Getting strung up if that mob outside gets its way. But I do know I'm going to need an attorney. There's a lawyer a couple of blocks down. Thacker, he's the only lawyer I know of.'

She pulled back. 'This is all that spiteful Louise's fault. She shouldn't have tittle-tattled the way she did. Sheriff Syson was an irritating man who enjoyed unsettling womenfolk. But it was just stupid talk.'

'He didn't speak to all women that way. You must have said something or acted in such a way to encourage him.'

'There was nothing between Sheriff Syson and me,' she said. 'You know that. But he was always pestering me. I didn't show him any encouragement.'

'You encourage men just by your manner. You've always appreciated the company of men more than that of women.'

She thought on it. 'I can't comment on that. Maybe it's true, but it's not intentional. You must believe me; there was nothing between us. You were, and are, the only one.'

There was a pause while he moved towards the conclusion. 'So I've killed a man for nothing.'

She pulled him to her. 'Don't talk that way, Fred.'

They were still huddled together when a detachment of soldiers came to take him to the fort.

Never having had any dealings with the law before, Hasty found himself in a complicated whirlwind of legalities. First was the coroner's inquest in which the doctor gave his opinion that the victim had died as a result of a broken neck.

The acting sheriff then gave his account of the circumstances. At the end, the coroner pointed out that the sole responsibility of his court was to ascertain the cause of death and not make decisions on culpability so Hasty was escorted back to the army guardhouse.

Next came a preliminary hearing to see if there was a case to answer. For this Hasty needed legal representation. Charlotte had failed to get the services of the experienced Thacker and, as Hasty knew of no others, the court appointed an attorney.

By the name of Fitzgerald, he was a young man with a purple birthmark across his cheek and mouth and when the fellow disclosed this was his first major case, Hasty's confidence hit rock bottom.

At the end of the hearing the judge decided there was a case to answer and the prosecutor demanded that the defendant be retained in custody. On the basis that his client had no previous record, Fitzgerald requested bail for his client, an action which caused an eruption amongst the spectators.

The judge rapped his gavel and pointed to the bailiff who bellowed, 'Order in court'.

Hasty couldn't understand the strength of the animosity against him. Maybe it was coming from Syson's family and friends; or maybe the townsfolk were simply turning on the man who had killed their local lawman.

The judge studied the crowd as it quietened, then rapped his gavel again. 'The defendant shall be retained in custody pending trial.'

It was a week later that the trial proper started. Hasty knew this was the big stuff now because, when the out-of-town judge swept in and mounted the bench, he wore a black robe. Up till then all officials had been local and in their ordinary work-a-day clothes.

The bailiff boomed, 'Court all rise'. Then, as folk settled into their seats the clerk of the court called the case, announcing in equally forbidding tones, 'Territory of Arizona v. Frederick Jones'.

As before, the first witnesses were the coroner and the doctor who repeated the findings of the inquest. Hasty felt a shudder when the prosecutor followed by reading out the charge of murder.

'If it please the court,' Hasty's attorney interjected, 'the defence would like to enter a plea of manslaughter.' From the start Hasty had never denied involving Syson in a fight or getting the better of him.

The judge pondered on it, looked through his papers and allowed the plea to run alongside the more serious charge. On the announcement, Fitzgerald winked at Hasty and for the first time the accused man began to get a little confidence in his young defender.

Then came an account of the events by the prosecutor, as he understood them. Various witnesses took the stand beginning with Sheriff Murray who explained how he had been called to the scene and had taken the defendant into custody. It was after Pete Lesley, the barman of the San Pedro, had given his testimony that Hasty's attorney made his next big contribution.

First he pointed out that Hasty had no record.

Then, during his questioning of the barman, he elicited from the man that Hasty had shown no intent of severely harming the deceased, other than venting his anger at what he saw was an affront. It was not the defendant's habit to wear guns and the confrontation had been just a matter of fists.

This seemed to go down OK until the prosecution brought forward a parade of other witnesses who attested to the fact that the defendant did have a history of temper. Despite his inexperience it was during this sequence that Fitzgerald showed at least he had a good knowledge of the law with his varied objections, many of which were sustained by the judge.

'So, I put it to you,' the prosecutor concluded, 'the prisoner in the dock is also a prisoner of his own mood and temper.'

'Don't take it personal,' Fitzgerald said, when he saw Hasty's face harden at the words. 'The guy's only doing his job. Now it's our turn.' And he called Mel Adams and a stream of character witnesses, each stating how the defendant was a hard-working, likeable fellow who generally got on with folks.

'Very well,' the judge said in summary, 'we get the point. We have a slightly flawed angel before us. Is there anything else you wish to add, Counsellor?'

Again Fitzgerald winked at Hasty before he stood up. 'The fact is, Your Honour, that Sheriff Syson was one of those men who saw every attractive woman as a challenge. There is no denying he cut a handsome figure, always closely shaved and neatly dressed. But he was a charmer who knew what women wanted to hear. Oozing compliments he had wormed his way into many a woman's bed.'

And he proved it with the line of witnesses he called to the stand. Unbeknown to his client he had been working overtime to marshal an army of women who had grievances against Syson.

'And it is rumoured,' he concluded 'that the philanderer has left at least one illegitimate child along the way.'

'Hearsay,' the judge snapped. 'Strike that from the record.'

Fitzgerald sat down, a smile touching the corners of his mouth. Although his conclusion had been stricken from the record, it had been heard by the jury, all local folk who knew it to be true.

And so it went on.

It was late afternoon when the proceedings moved towards a conclusion with Fitzgerald making a final plea for lenience on the basis that the defendant had had a justifiable grievance against the deceased. This was not the first time that Syson had pestered his wife with his discourteous advances. 'Thus my client acted in the heat of the moment. Of course he was wrong to take the law into his own hands, and he fully acknowledges that.'

The jury were out for only a short while, coming back with the finding of 'guilty of manslaughter'. Then followed a recess while the judge considered the case and the appropriate sentence.

On his return Hasty was ordered to stand. 'I am of the opinion,' the judge said, 'that there was no intent on your part to kill the late Sheriff Syson. So, in fixing the sentence, I am taking that into account along with the fact that till now you have had a clean record. On the other hand, you are a young man who must learn to curb his impulses. A man has died as the result of your lack of restraint and for that you will serve a total of four years. That is, with credit for the time you have already served while awaiting trial. Consequently you will be taken from this court to the nearest place of confinement, there to await transportation to the territorial penitentiary.'

'Four years?' Hasty shouted. 'For an accident?'

'Counsel,' the judge snapped, 'restrain your client.'

The court rose again and it was all over.

'Four years?' Hasty repeated to his attorney as he slumped into his seat and the room began to empty. 'Four years for an accident? Can we appeal?'

'I suggest not,' the young man said. 'You have to remember, it has not been deemed an accident, it's manslaughter. The fact is, you did very well here, Mr Jones. I don't think you could have hoped for a better deal from the judge. It's manslaughter, not murder. You didn't draw the hangman's noose. So, before you ask me to seek an appeal, bear in mind a higher court could reverse that decision.'

Hasty checked his impulses. Calming down he shook the man's hand, coming to the realization that the young greenhorn had done a good job. And with that, the convicted man was manacled again and led away.

Chained to other prisoners, Hasty shuffled through the Sallyport Gate, the arch that marked the entrance to Yuma Territorial Prison. The new intake were hosed down and given prison denims. They were assembled in the yard where they were addressed by the warden.

'This is your official welcome to the establishment which is to be your home for the duration of whatever sentence the courts deemed fitting to the particular malfeasance you perpetrated. But mark, it will not be a home from home. We are not paid by the Territory of Arizona to make your stay a pleasant one. Just remember from this day on you are just scum with a number and those amongst you who seek trouble will get trouble. Seeking trouble starts with Rule One: you do not speak to a member of my staff unless spoken to. There are many other rules but you will learn them the hard way. However, we are not unreasonable custodians. If you follow orders without question, your discomforts will be minimized.'

But that was not strictly true.

On the second day he was taken from his cell into the yard where there was a cart bearing a corpse and shovel. His ankles were manacled and he was ordered to push the cart through the gate.

He had noticed the cemetery as the prison wagon had rolled in, just outside to the east. Simple piles of rocks marked the graves, just the width and height of the dead prisoners below; each pile had a plain slab on which was scratched a name. Hasty was ordered to dig two holes. When he had lowered the body into one and covered it in, he stood leaning on the shovel. 'Who's the other one for?'

The guard whacked him across the jaw with his stick. 'Didn't you hear the warden? You don't speak unless you are spoken to.'

Hasty's impulse was to lash out, but he diverted his anger into gripping the shovel harder.

'Go on,' the guard grinned, noting the tension. 'Just try to, son. We'd love you to try it.'

Hasty looked at the swinging stick of the guard and the levelled gun of his companion behind him, and gripped his shovel even harder.

'Now the warden has had his say we have ours,' his attacker went on. 'Fact is, there are certain kinds of con we just don't take kindly to. Child molesters, perverts. But most of all, we don't like any killer of a brother law officer.' He gestured at the vacant hole with his stick. 'That other's for you, lawman killer. Remember that – when you're trying to sleep at night. Listen to the crickets out here. They'll be calling for you. You got four years of our company. Lots of time to give us reason to put you in it.'

Back inside he was taken to an isolated room where the guards continued having their 'say' – with their heavy sticks.

# THREE

'How much you got in your poke?'

Hasty Jones pondered on the matter. 'Figure there was about fifty dollars in my wallet when they took it off me.'

'Well, with the ten dollars the state gives you to see you on your way, that makes a grand total of sixty. Ain't much to take back to your wife and kid.'

Hasty shrugged. 'Ain't much I can do about that sack of potatoes.'

'Oh, yes there is.'

'Oh, yeah. I can work my ass for a month and take back a few more dollars. But I want to see my family as soon as possible, no matter how little I got in my pocket. That's my main aim, you know that.'

'Hell, you can get good money a lot quicker than that.'

Hasty eyed his companion contemplatively. 'Listen, I'm just coming to the end of three years. Ain't no way I'm gonna jeopardize my future by some half-ass criminal shenanigans as soon as I'm out.'

The other smiled. 'Don't worry, my friend. I'm talking about something straight-up legit.' Thomas Deeds was the name on the prison roster but the little man was known to all as Eight-Ball. The lethargic appearance suggested by his slightly hunched shoulders was countered by the wide-awake eyes. 'It'll just take a couple of days is all,' he continued, 'and you'll pull at least a hundred.'

'A hundred? That's more than a month's hard sweat last time I knew anything about earning a wage. Ain't no way a guy can pull that kind of money in a couple of days by honest means.'

Eight-Ball grinned. 'Must say, for a diehard criminal you sure don't know much about the workings of the world.' He stood up and went to the bars. 'Hey, Elmo. Can we borrow your deck of cards?'

Normally the request would have been met by scorn. With its inevitability of violence, card playing amongst the prisoners was strictly forbidden. But the two men were due to be released and for their remaining weeks they had been placed together in a holding cell. It was the convention that rules were relaxed for long-term inmates preparing for departure; and they were fed good meals so they would present an air of healthiness to the outside world. Especially to the local do-gooders who were always looking for reasons to complain about prison conditions.

From his desk the turnkey eyed them. He'd known

the two inmates long enough to know they were friends and not likely to bilk each other out of their leaving cash. He opened the drawer of his desk and withdrew a deck of cards which he brought over and passed through the bars to the prisoner. 'Just for amusement,' he warned. 'Not for money. Leastways not serious money. No point in starting your new lives broke and hating each other.'

'Understood,' Eight-Ball said. 'You can watch if you like.' He returned to the small table in the cell and riffle-shuffled the deck. 'You OK with blackjack, Mr Jones?'

'Never been much of a card man. That what they call Twenty-One?'

'Yeah. Got lotsa names. The Limeys call it pontoon.'

Hasty hauled himself off his bunk and joined his companion at the table. 'Yeah, I've played. What's your idea?'

Eight-Ball emptied a box of matches and divided them into two equal piles. 'OK, you be the dealer. Deal to me and a couple of dummy hands to make like there's three punters at the table in some fancy casino.'

Hasty dealt the cards as prescribed.

'The only rule you follow as dealer,' Eight-Ball said, studying his cards, 'is that you hit if you're below seventeen.'

'Hit?'

'Draw another card.'

Play ensued until, twenty minutes later, the little man had taken all the matches. He asked the jailer for another box, the contents of which he also divided equally. Play recommenced and half an hour on he had all the matches stacked before him.

Hasty sat back, made a smoke and used one of the matches to light it. 'Hell, how did you do it? You're cheating, but I just can't see how.'

Eight-Ball laughed. 'No, I ain't cheating.'

'Well, you just had a good run of luck.'

'Yeah, that helps – but not luck in the way you think. You see, it's a matter of watching the cards. Science in a way, I suppose. For starters, at the end of a game you know the value of maybe eight cards. If you're lucky, you know more. You know what you were dealt and what the dealer had.' He nodded to the two dummy hands. 'Plus any others that were exposed during the hand.'

'So?' Hasty challenged. 'Anybody with the two eyes God gave him can see that.'

Eight-Ball touched the side of his forehead. 'Yeah, but you gotta use something else the good Lord gave you: memory. What you gotta look out for is when there's a lot of high cards in a bunch coming through. So, you play low stakes while you count the cards during successive games until the high bunch reappear at the top of the deck. See, house rule is up to seventeen the dealer has to hit, so when there's a bunch of high cards sitting on the top of his deck he's gonna bust more often. That's when you raise your bets.'

'But it's not a dead cert that he's gonna draw a *high* card.'

'Of course not, you bozo. But the *odds* are he will and, over time, you'll be a net winner.'

'What happens if the dealer shuffles?'

'Well, a beginner like you has to start counting again.'

'And what about somebody who's not a beginner, like you?'

'I watch the shuffle. I can usually track a string of high cards with a normal shuffle. But a real good player can track a bunch of a dozen cards through a six-deck shuffle without breaking a sweat.'

He redistributed the matches into equal piles and took the deck. 'Now I'll be the dealer and you be the punter.'

Some hour and a half on, the smell of dinner permeated the air as their meals were brought in. By which time Hasty had nearly all the matches.

'Hey, ain't all that difficult, is it?' he said, an air of triumph in his voice, as they settled down to their meal. 'Like you say, all you need is a pair of eyes and a good memory. Can't see why more don't play the system.'

Eight-Ball put a gravy-covered potato into his mouth. 'First off, most folks don't know it. The bulk of punters are no-accounts who have just wandered in off the streets to chance a dollar. Even if they do have some idea how to play the odds, a guy's gotta have the sand to play big and not to fold when he's hitting a low run. Your run-of-the–mill punter ain't got that level of guts. Then, of course, they're close to a bar and the barleycorn will be flowing. Get enough booze down your throat while you're playing and you might have trouble remembering where you live, never mind a long sequence of cards.'

Hasty finished off a biteful of meat. 'If it's so easy, why do you bother with horse-rustling and stuff? That's what got you in here.'

'Ah, there's the rub, my friend. See, the boss of a gaming house, he knows the signs of the game. Now you're getting into the swing of it, you've learned enough to know that you play low and you only up the ante when you know the high bunch is coming through again. Dealers ain't greenhorns. Any dealer worth his salt will spot a guy playing like that and he knows what's going on. Then, when you start winning regular, even without cheating, he'll bar you from his tables. So you gotta move on to the next parlour or town. Trouble is the percentage advantage is so small that it takes time. For quick money there's a bigger pay-off from hoss- and cattle-rustling.'

'That's if you don't get caught.'

Eight-Ball chuckled. 'Yeah. Ain't there a drawback to everything?' For a while he concentrated on eating. After years on swill, a good meal was something you relished. 'So,' he said at the end of the feast, 'this suggestion of mine, about dabbling in the pasteboards a spell before you hit the trail for home – you game?'

Hasty nodded reflectively as he rolled a cigarette. 'OK, but where?'

'Yuma City. No place like what's been our backyard these past years.'

Hasty looked puzzled. 'Yuma? I only caught a glimpse of the place when they first brought me in, but I saw enough to know it's just a collection of rundown adobes by the river. That's unless it's growed a mite in three years.'

The other smiled. 'See, you being a dirt farmer, you just ain't travelled. No matter how small, every place that man settles will have its brothels and swingdoor saloons providing for elemental needs – even a pissant place like Yuma.'

Hasty fired his cigarette, lay down on his bunk and watched the smoke waft upwards. 'Yeah, a few extra dollars won't come amiss.'

'OK, pal, we got three days left. Three days to get you playing the system like a natural.'

# FOUR

'Well, I beat the bastards,' Hasty Jones said to himself as he walked once more through Sallyport Gate, the arch that marked the entrance to Yuma Territorial Prison.

But more important for him now – the entrance marked the exit.

Behind him, a lock clanked shut. He stepped out of the shade of the adobe walls and noted the cemetery. It was only the second time he had seen the graveyard since his incarceration. There were never any mourners at the perfunctory burials. But that first time, three years ago, was scored indelibly in his brain.

As he passed he didn't look closely but he knew he would be familiar with a lot of the names, fellow prisoners who had died during his three-year stretch. Most had died of consumption, which had a habit of spreading quickly in the densely packed quarters. He was well aware that he could have been with them

41

there under the caliche – but, in his case, consumption probably wouldn't have been the cause.

Whenever the screws beat him, starved him, or threw him into solitary for the slightest reason, he would be reminded there was a slab with his name on it just outside, ready, waiting.

The scars from the wounds inflicted on him would stay with him for the rest of his life. And there were other physical signs of his time spent in the cramped 8 by 10 foot cells: more lines on his face, hair beginning to thin, touches of grey.

But there were stronger muscles too. The jail had been under continuous construction since its opening and the only labour used was that of the convicts such as he. Coupled with the poor diet, hard physical toil had been too much for some, but for Hasty Jones hard work had served to maintain his body.

Moreover, the changes were not only physical. He was different inside. Stronger mentally. He had learned control. It had been his temper that had got him into the hell hole that was Yuma Pen, and he knew it would keep him longer away from his beloved family should he let his temper rip again. So he had taken whatever crap the screws had thrown at him. It had been difficult but he had managed it. So much so that eventually he even got a commendation of parole from the warden himself – with a year off his sentence.

He followed Eight-Ball up through the back door into the prison wagon. The mobile cage was on its way to pick up prisoners at Yuma City and the newly released men had been offered a lift to town.

As he sat down, Eight-Ball winked. Both remained silent as they pulled away and Hasty glanced through the barred windows. For a second the iron rods made him conscious of being caged again but the feeling soon dissipated. The last time he had been in the vehicle he had been shackled. Now, three years on, his hands were free and the guard had closed the door behind them *without* locking it. Little things like that he noticed.

He took a last look at the cemetery – the boneyard that so many screws had aimed to make his last resting place. 'Yes, sir,' he repeated to himself, 'I beat the bastards.'

As they approached the town he could see steamboats coming down the Colorado. The wagon lurched to a standstill on the main drag and they stepped down.

'Now you guys behave yourselves,' the guard said. 'Folks hereabouts know all about freed cons letting rip and they ain't partial to it. Any boozing and hoorahing you feel like doing, leave it until you're out of their bailiwick. Otherwise you'll simply exchange the Pen for the local hoosegow. Best of luck, fellers.'

'They ain't all bastards,' Hasty concluded, as he watched the guard go off to collect his new batch of prisoners.

'If you say so,' his companion said, 'but let's get out of here. Ain't exactly gonna raise my spirits getting a close look-see at the poor critters who are taking our place.'

Hasty looked across the river and could see Fort Yuma, the original basis for the town, perched on a hill on the western bank. Then they walked down the street, not speaking, both simply enjoying watching folk go about their day-to-day business. Even more, they were revelling in the fact they could stand, sit, walk, smoke, go for a piss whenever they wanted.

They passed adobes, unkempt-looking buildings made of wattle and daub, ramshackle fences made of ocotillo ribs.

'You sure we'll be able to pick up our grubstake playing cards in this place?' Hasty asked after some minutes. 'Sure don't look like the kind of place where's there's money to be had for the taking.'

'Trust me,' Eight-Ball said. 'Let's find ourselves a place where we can lay our heads, then we'll head downtown.'

Eight-Ball was right. After they'd established digs in a place run by a Mexican couple and taken a filling meal of *frijoles* and *tortillas*, they started the evening by exploring the downtown area and soon saw they had a selection of cantinas and gaming parlours from which to choose.

Once they had the lie of the place, they worked separately except for the first saloon they went into, where Hasty played while Eight-Ball stayed in the background to give him moral support. When he could see Hasty was in the swing of it, he gave his partner a surreptitious signal that he was leaving and then went to plough his own furrow.

Towards midnight, they met up outside one of the liquor houses and leant on the boardwalk rail.

'How did you do?' Eight-Ball asked.

'Twenty dollars up. Was a mite hairy to start with. It's a tad different playing for real.'

'Don't fret. Twenty ain't bad for a beginner. I'm proud of you.'

'And you?'

'Ain't totalled it up exactly but something like sixty. Come on, I'll buy you a drink out of my winnings.' He nodded to the place behind them. 'It don't matter if we're seen together in here. They ain't got gaming tables. With the night's work over we can relax a spell.'

Inside they selected a table out of earshot of the few remaining customers. 'Now, you've wet your feet,' Eight-Ball said in a low voice when they were settled with their drinks, 'tomorrow we play as a team. I'll be the major player and you sit at the same table, playing minimum bets. It's the same principle but we push the advantages further in our favour by you letting me know what's in your hand plus what you might see of other hands.'

'How do I do that?'

'We'll work out a simple set of codes, movements,

words, things which come natural to you. With the additional information, the string of high cards that we are looking for can get up to fifteen cards. That means I can raise bets higher than if I was just counting by myself.'

'Ain't this cheating?'

'Hell, no. It's like I've told you. It's all a matter of watching and having a good memory. And, as we're a team, we'll split the take.'

The next night went even better. That is, until part way through the evening.

They were sitting adjacent at the same table and the system of codes was working well as evidenced by the pile of coins and bills in front of Eight-Ball. During the present state of play he had been placing low bets when Hasty's scratching of his left ear confirmed his own judgement that a high run was coming up.

He noted the dealer's total of fifteen making the conditions just right. The dealer had to draw. Eight-Ball put twenty dollars on his nine and a deuce and pointed his finger at the table, the convention for requesting another card. He picked it up: a knave, which gave him the required twenty-one. He waved his hand, signalling he was sticking.

The dealer pulled a queen, putting him over the top. He scowled and pushed forward two ten-spots and some coins which Eight-Ball added to the stack of money in front of him.

'New deck,' the dealer announced.

'If it's OK with you, sir,' Eight-Ball said, 'I'll take advantage of the break in play to take a leak. Which way's the john?'

The dealer gestured to the back, and Eight-Ball gathered his winnings and left his seat.

Hasty leant back and took a swig of his drink, but then noticed an exchange of glances between the dealer and a well-dressed man at the bar whom he had judged to be the owner. The man nodded to a big man at his side and they both headed for the back.

Things didn't look good. Hasty emptied his glass. 'I'll get a refill,' he said, rising and making a show of heading for the bar and another drink. 'Same again,' he said to the barman. But as he placed his glass on the counter he turned and headed for the back.

As he approached the door he heard a voice outside. 'You're a no-good cheat. I want my money back.'

Opening the door he saw it was the owner speaking while the heavy had a gun levelled at Eight-Ball.

'I ain't no four-flusher, mister,' Eight-Ball said. 'I'm winning fair and square.'

'Like hell you are,' the man snarled.

Hasty staggered noisily out of the light into the darkness as though drunk. The owner turned. 'You – stay out of this.' The man gestured to the fence that marked the privy. 'Do what you have to do and get back inside.'

Hasty lurched forward. It was clear he and his friend hadn't been tagged as working as a pair. 'Yes, sir,' he slurred, touching his forelock, 'ain't none of my business, boss. I ain't seed nothing.' He maintained his drunken stagger for a moment as he headed for the privy, then suddenly he lunged at the man with the gun. The force of his hurtling body sent both men tumbling to the dirt.

Simultaneously the diminutive Eight-Ball leapt at the owner, swinging an uppercut such that the man's head bounced back from the blow.

Having the advantage because he had hit the gunman with all his weight, Hasty managed to get on top of his opponent. He grabbed the man's wrist and slammed it against the ground. The man's fingers popped open releasing the gun, but he hooked his other fist at his attacker's jaw. Hasty's head jerked back with the punch. But he had taken much worse in prison and he returned a fist that crashed the man's head to one side.

Meanwhile the owner, now also on the ground, grappled in his jacket pocket and pulled a derringer. Eight-Ball lashed out with his boot and knocked the weapon from the man's hand.

Assessing his own opponent to be out, Hasty slowly got to his feet and stood on shaky legs. He picked up the gun and slung it as far as he could into the darkness. He breathed hard to catch his breath and looked at Eight-Ball.

He was standing over the downed owner. 'Like I

said. I ain't no cheat, mister. You just don't like losing.' Then he hurled the derringer into the blackness and gestured with his head to his companion that they should leave.

'We won't go straight back to our diggings in case the bozo sends someone to follow us,' he said as they jogged down the alley. 'We'll make a detour round the town.'

Finally, having ensured they weren't being followed, they headed back to their quarters. 'Well, pardner, looks like our Yuma days are over,' he said. 'Best we leave town first thing tomorrow. And thanks for helping me out back there.'

'Hell's teeth, Eight-Ball, I don't need thanks. We were working as a team, remember?'

'Well, I owe you one.'

'How did the guy twig to what was going on?'

'Don't think he did. Didn't cotton to parting with his money is all. Just our luck to run into a bozo like him.' He grinned. 'Like I said, ain't there a drawback to everything?'

# FIVE

Next morning they were standing by the bank of the Colorado looking west across the river. Eight-Ball's estimate had been right and Hasty was returning home with over a hundred extra bucks in his pocket.

'What are your plans now?' Hasty asked. He had made enquiries about the schedule of the eastbound stage and now, at the appointed time, they were near the jetty waiting for the ferry. Eight-Ball had said he would hang around until he had seen his companion safely on his way.

'Dunno. But whatever it is, it'll be straight. I tell you, feller, I don't cotton to another spell in the pen. Suppose I'll bum around until something turns up. I got kin in California. They got a place growing oranges and stuff. Might travel out and see if they've got anything going.'

He rummaged through his pockets as he spoke, then adding, 'Hey, you got the makings? I'm out.'

A crumpled envelope was inadvertently in Hasty's

hand as he pulled out his tobacco pouch. He handed the makings to his companion and opened the envelope. Then he recognized it as a scrawled message from a friend asking to see him when he came out – he had forgotten about it – and he slipped it back in his pocket while he waited for the return of the tobacco so he could make his own cigarette.

Eventually they saw the stage roll up on the other side of the river. In silence they shared a last cigarette together as they watched the coach being unharnessed and rolled on to the ferry. At the completion of the crossing fresh horses were added.

'Reckon this is it, pal,' Hasty said, grabbing Eight-Ball's shoulder and shaking his hand.

The other responded warmly and they made their goodbyes and in no time at all, courtesy of Mr Butterfield, Hasty was bouncing his way to Maricopa Wells, the line's sling station that marked the halfway point back to Tucson.

All he could think of now was Charlotte – Charley as he called her – and little Jimmy. Despite all that had happened to him behind the iron bars, missing his wife and kid had been the worst part of prison. Had she changed? She had visited him a couple of times in the early days. That was before the screws realized that that was another way of getting at him and had engineered reasons why she couldn't come. But he adjusted mentally to that too, compensating himself with the thought that it was far too long, costly and dangerous a journey to do regularly, especially a lone female.

Wood creaked, springs squeaked and hoofs thumped the ground. He looked longingly out of the window as the coach rolled across the harsh, flat land. For three years the face of his wife and child had slid through his mind. Charley, the full lips, the pert nose, the way she moved the wisps of hair away from her sparkly hazel eyes as she toiled in the kitchen, the expression on her sleeping face; and the boy's young, unformed face, his eyes, with the same colour and vivacity as his mother's, eagerly taking in the world.

It would not be long before he would be with them again.

The coach duly made Maricopa Wells. 'Leaving in ten minutes, folks,' the driver said, hauling on the brake. Ostlers set about unharnessing the horses while the passengers filed into the 'dobe building for refreshment.

Inside, they were greeted by a Mexican couple who tended to their needs. Impatient to be on his way, Hasty made do with a glass of lemonade and took it to the door to watch fresh horses being led out of the corral.

'Hey,' he shouted after a while, when he seemed to recognize one the men fiddling with the harness. 'Ain't that Jez Hollins?'

'Sure is, feller,' the man responded, looking up. 'Who's asking?'

Hasty stepped from the veranda and crossed the alkali dust.

The man shielded his eyes with his hand. 'Well, if it ain't Hasty Jones. Ain't seen you for a long spell.'

'Three years or more.'

'Ah, yeah,' the man said, remembering. 'How long you been out?'

'Couple of days. I'm on my way home now.'

'Well, good to see you, pal.'

'What are you doing out here?'

The man chuckled. 'I'm your driver.'

Hasty gestured to the upfront seat. 'You been there all the while?'

'Yeah, all the way from Yuma.'

'Didn't recognise you before.'

'Likewise, pal.'

'Say, it OK for me to sit with you up on the box for the remainder of the journey?'

'No problem.'

A couple of hours on, Hasty began to recognize the terrain as the trail cut through the land of the Cruz Cattle Company.

'Now I know I'm getting near home,' he said. 'I used to punch for the Triple C.'

'I didn't know that.'

'Yeah. Worked for Old Ben Matthews for several years when I was a younker.' From the early days the Cruz had been the biggest outfit in Pima County. 'That's before I got married and started my own homestead.'

'I remember Old Ben. Been gone a few years now.'

'I didn't know.' Then, adding, 'I suppose there are lots of changes I've got to get used to.'

The coach lurched along before turning off the trail.

'Hey, where are we going?' Hasty asked, unhappy that the coach seemed to be making a detour.

'Don't fret,' Jez chuckled. 'I won't keep you from your missus longer than necessary. Won't be long. Just checking to see if the Triple C's got any mail.'

'Ah, yes. I was forgetting.'

The *casa principal* with its large adobe-covered forecourt rang chords of familiarity for the returning traveller. Near the hitch rails, the mounting block he had built for Old Ben to use before his legs finally went. But there was something strange about the place, something forlorn. Apart from the clanking windmill there was little activity; certainly not the bustle that Hasty remembered from the working cattle outfit. Few horses dotted about the corrals and hardly any men visible amongst the spread of structures: from the bunkhouse to the stable and barns. But he paid little heed, having other things on his mind.

The homestead being only a short distance from the main trail he arranged with Jez to be dropped off before they hit town. As he stepped down he heard a haunting distant drone.

'What's that?' he asked.

The driver pointed in the direction of Tucson.

'That's the afternoon train.'

'Train?' Hasty looked and saw a smudge of black smoke. 'Well, I'll be. Things have sure changed around here.'

'Like you were saying, there's gonna be lots of changes you're gonna notice. Three years away? Hell, you might as well have been living on the moon.' He flicked the ribbons to depart. 'See you, pal.'

As he waved goodbye, Hasty repeated the notion in his mind. 'The moon? Yeah, seems I might well have been.' And with that he started the last lap of his return home.

Striding through the alkali dust he watched the homestead gradually take shape through the heat-haze before him, a little oasis of green in a parched, dun land. And, as the place became more distinct, signs of his long absence also became clear. The outer fields were unploughed. Grass, usually trimmed for horse feed, was waist-high. Nearer, he noted corral posts needed fixing. Closer, he could see paint was peeling from the porch.

Charlotte was working in the potato field when he saw her. As he approached he took off his hat. The sound of his slapping the dust out of it caught her attention.

At first she was unbelieving then, gasping his name, dropped the spade and ran to him.

He took her in his arms. 'It's great to be back,' he whispered.

After a while, they held each other at a distance, exploring each other's features for signs of the passage of time. Her auburn hair was drawn back, held by a band of patterned cloth. New lines were etched at the corners of her eyes, edges of her mouth.

For a spell, words only used by lovers passed between them. Then, with arms wrapped round each other, they strolled to the house.

'Where's Jimmy?' he asked.

'Today's a school day. He'll be back later.'

In the yard he pumped up some fresh water and splashed the alkali dust from his face.

'That's my Hasty,' she said, noting the face that had now appeared from under the coating of grime. 'Come on. I'm going to prepare us a royal slap-up meal.'

He followed her as she stepped up into the house. In front of the porch, the flower patch of which his wife had been proud was now sorry-looking and weed-strangled. In his absence she had had more important things to do. At least the vegetables in the kitchen garden were looking healthy. She knew her priorities.

In the kitchen, she made to prepare coffee; but he came up behind her, picked her up bodily and strode towards the bedroom.

'What time did you say Jimmy comes back?'

It was late afternoon when a neighbour's buggy delivered the young lad back home from school.

'I've got a surprise,' Charley said to her son by way of greeting.

Hasty was snoozing on the horsehair sofa when the boy entered. The words, 'Your pa's home,' woke the man.

He blinked open his eyes. In other circumstances he might not have recognized his son. At least a foot taller and the puppy fat of his face was gone.

He hauled himself into a sitting position and held out his arms to hug and kiss him the way he used to. But the boy held back and it took a couple of seconds for it to dawn on the returning father that hugging and kissing was something the growing man had probably now left behind him.

So he made do with shaking his hand and patting the sofa for the lad to sit beside him. 'Come here. Tell me about yourself.'

It was too wide a question and the boy looked blank. Besides, the figure sitting next to him had become a distant memory, somebody his ma talked about but who had no physical being. This man beside him was flesh and blood, rough-skinned, hairy-handed and stubble-chinned. And with a smell that was strange. Now accustomed only to the close presence of his mother with her scents and womanly aromas, the young lad didn't realize that this strangeness was merely the smell of a man.

Later they took their meal with candles on the table. The meal was accompanied by much noise and

Jimmy eventually opened up joining in the general babble: laughter, the signs of gaiety, but interspersed with awkward stretches of silence.

After a chat around the fire, Hasty took Jimmy to his bedroom, the lean-to he had added to the side of the main building many years ago. They spoke for a while, man and boy beginning to relate once more, and after goodnights had been exchanged and the lamp extinguished Hasty leant down and kissed his son's forehead in the darkness.

The couple sat for a while, silently watching the dying embers of the fire. Eventually, hearing his snoring, Charley helped her husband into bed.

She locked up, climbed under the sheets beside him then doused the kerosene. But, lying for a moment alone, he had been disturbed by the noises that she had been making. Without speaking, he rose and returned to the outside door. He unlocked it, opened it and looked at the night sky for a moment. Closing the door but not locking it, he returned.

'What's the matter, Hasty?' she asked, as he clambered back into bed.

'Don't think I'm ever gonna get used to hearing a lock being closed behind me again.'

# SIX

The next morning Charley let him sleep in, so the sun was high in the sky when he finally awoke. He took it easy till lunchtime, then spent the afternoon looking over the place, taking stock of what needed doing. He did the odd job here and there but when he looked through his tools he found his store of nails and screws had rusted up. While he did what repairs he could, Jimmy was always within speaking or hailing distance, but the lad seemed preoccupied with his own thoughts. He would answer the occasional question that Hasty threw his way but never initiated any discussion. There was no surliness in his manner but he showed reluctance to enter into any conversation.

'Jimmy's quiet about me,' Hasty said, in a low voice to his wife when they were alone in the kitchen that evening washing the dishes.

'You've got to understand. He's been through a lot. The local kids have given him a rough time. You know how cruel children can be sometimes. He does-n't talk about it now but when you first went away he told me how they were turning on him. Then, after school, they stopped inviting him over to play, and turned down invitations for them to come and play over here.'

'Kids,' he muttered.

'I think the cold-shouldering was as much to do with their parents,' she added.

Hasty studied the plate he had just dried. 'Poor little feller.'

'Besides,' she added, 'you're almost a stranger now. In a way he's got to get to know you again. You've got to bear that in mind. Give him time.'

'Figure he blames me for providing the kids with something to torment him about. The son of a killer.' He put down the cloth. 'Give us a few minutes alone, honey. I'll have a word with him.'

Back in the front room, Jimmy was sitting at the table with pencil stub in hand and concentrating closely on a piece of paper.

Hasty looked over the lad's shoulder and saw a drawing of a horse. 'Hey, you're quite an artist, Jimmy. That there rendering of a hoss is better than I could do *now*.'

He moved over to the sofa and patted the space beside him. 'Come and sit with your pa for a while.'

Jimmy put down his pencil and, head down in the way of children reluctantly obeying, he crossed the room.

'It must have been bad for you at school,' Hasty said, as the boy hesitantly took up the indicated place. 'I mean, kids ribbing you about me and all.'

'I got used it.'

Hasty nodded, suddenly not knowing what next to say.

There was a silence, then Jimmy asked, 'Why did you do it, Dad? You know, the thing they put you away for.'

Hasty hadn't expected such a direct question and his mind raced. Then, 'You ever done something you wished you hadn't?'

The boy paused and then voiced a hesitant, 'Yes.'

'Well, same with me. If I could turn the clock back I would, Jimmy. If I hadn't done what I done, it would have saved you and your ma a lot of grief. Not to mention me. But I can't turn the clock back. Fact of life. What's done is done.'

'Yes, but *why* did you do it?'

The man thought about it and tried a different tack. 'You know my name's Fred but most folks don't call me that.'

'No, they call you Hasty Jones.'

'You know what hasty means?'

The boy pulled an exaggeratedly wry look. 'No.'

'It means doing things on the spur of the moment, without thinking. I must have been born like it. Anyways, whenever I did anything quickly at school the teacher would call me "Hasty". My classmates picked it up and it stuck. But you see, trouble is, one of the things that makes a fellow act hasty is a temper. And a quick temper is something I've always been saddled with.'

'You lost your temper with the sheriff?'

'Yeah. Wrong thing to do but I did.'

He wanted to be open with his son but realized he was still too young for some details. He wanted to tell him the kind of man Sheriff Syson had been. About the several occasions when in town, and leaving Charley to do her shopping while he went about his own business, he had come across the varmint turning on the snake-oil charm with his ma. And at such times there had been an exchange of words between the two men. And on each occasion, with his glib use of words, the sheriff had made Hasty look a boorish oaf in front of his wife and onlookers; a yokel too uncouth to understand what was merely polite conversation.

He wanted to explain how on the fateful day, his mother had gone to town without him. How the sheriff had made an obscene comment to her, which had been the last straw. And how one thing had led to another.

But he could relate none of these details to his son. He coughed and said, 'See, son, him and me, we had a . . . a . . . disagreement. In my temper, I sought him out and deliberately picked a fight. When we started smashing into each other, I saw red. There are times I don't know my own strength; next thing he was lying dead on the ground.'

'It was something to do with ma, wasn't it?'

Hasty remained silent for a moment. He was a fool to think that Jimmy wouldn't have heard something in three years: town gossip, tongues wagging.

'You mom's OK, kid. She's a good woman. Don't let anybody tell you different. It was me that was at fault.'

The silence returned and Hasty concluded enough had been said for the moment. He stood up, crossed the room and appraised the drawing. 'You like drawing and stuff?'

'Yes, sir,' Jimmy said, joining him.

'You sure got some flair. What colour you gonna make this bronc?'

'I don't have anything to colour it with, sir.'

'You haven't? Well, I'll tell you what, Jimmy. You and me'll go to town tomorrow and buy some paints or crayons, something to colour it with. You like that?'

'Yes, sir.'

Hasty patted the top of the boy's head and then returned to the kitchen to rejoin his wife. 'I have to go to town tomorrow, to get nails and stuff,' he told her. 'I'll take Jimmy with me.'

He lowered his voice. 'Just the two of us. It might give us a chance to break some ice. You know, just a lad and his old man.'

'Good idea. I'll make sandwiches.'

# SEVEN

Next morning, his face scrubbed, Jimmy was eagerly waiting in the driving seat of their wagon. Hasty fastened the tailgate then climbed up to join his son. Waving a farewell he clucked the team and they began to roll.

The sun was warm and the going good. Jimmy was already losing some of his reticence and Hasty felt happier.

In time they could see the familiar shape of The San Xavier del Bac, the mission known as the White Dove of the Desert, gleaming in the sun and marking their proximity to town. But when they had passed Fort Lowell with its distant harsh memories and were entering the town proper, the passage of the years became obvious to Hasty's ears and eyes: the hooting of the locomotive as it worked up a head of steam out of town; then there were more buildings, big ones with wide patios and long-shaded porches.

But the familiar stuff was there too: miners, Mexicans and mantillas.

Familiar faces too. A couple gave a flicker of a smile but most became heavy-faced on recognition and, after a few such guarded interchanges, he gave up on touching his hat to folk.

He drew the wagon up beside the boardwalk.

'Look after things, Son,' he said, as he dropped down. 'I'll only be a shake. Then we'll find a candy store.' He mounted the boardwalk and walked down a block, each stride carrying him past more accusing eyes.

Reaching the law office door, he knocked. Although he had told Charley about getting supplies there was another reason why he had to go to Tuscon, but he hadn't wanted to concern her with it.

Sheriff Murray looked up as he came in. The face behind the desk was vague remembrance. The lined cheeks that gave them a grain like weathered board. The woolly sideburns down to his jaw-line. But the lines in the grain were deeper and the rampant sideburns were now streaked with grey. Time took its toll, even for those not in prison.

Behind him a young rangy man wearing a deputy's badge was leaning on one hip, a coffee mug in his hand.

On the wall between them, a board chequered with Wanted posters.

The sheriff was chewing tobacco and his jaw slacked in its action when he saw Hasty. 'What the—?'

he grunted, surprise and displeasure equally manifest in his face. 'Hasty Jones? What the hell are you doing out? Four years haven't passed that quick, have they?'

Hasty looked past the seated man to the corridor leading to the jail. From his position he could see the cell where he had been kept while they had waited for the troops from Fort Lowell to collect him. Three years on, looked like the same dirty paliasse on the cot, and the same pisspot.

'Got parole.'

'Parole?' the sheriff echoed.

'Yeah. I been a good boy.'

'Huh,' the sheriff snorted, 'parole for "good behaviour"? You – parole?'

'That's what they call it.'

The sheriff slipped his chewing tobacco to one side so that his cheek bulged. 'Well, left to me, three years ain't enough for killing a fellow lawman.'

'It ain't left to you.'

'And why the hell are you showing your face in here? You got nerve.'

Hasty took a paper from his pocket and waved it. 'Nothing to do with nerve, Sheriff. Got a document here that says I have to report to the local law officer once a week. Figure that means you.' He smiled. 'It also means we're gonna be seeing each other regular – whether you like it or not.'

The sheriff looked it over, a hard smile coming to his lips. 'OK, Jones, but just remember, we're gonna be watching you. Me and' – he thumbed towards the young man at his side – 'Deputy Clayton here. The slightest trouble and you'll be back inside. Yuma Pen if I have anything to do with it. Then maybe the guys back there can finish the job.' He handed back the paper. 'All right, I seen you. Now vamoose.'

Hasty headed for the door ruminating on how a piece of tin could turn a no-account bastard into a real bastard. Outside he leant on the rail, momentarily forgetting Jimmy waiting down the block. Unaware of the folks huddling and pointing his way, he put together a cigarette. Seeing the jail in the office took his mind back to when Charley visited him just after his arrest. His mind had still been twisted with anger. Anger with Charley, anger with the world.

He remembered the two of them huddled in the bald, stinking cell; and the words that came out. So I've killed a man for nothing: the words that had racketed around his head for three years. Stupid words. He'd had no intention of killing Syson. It had just fell that way.

Suddenly he remembered Jimmy and forced a smile for his son as he returned to the wagon. 'Come on, kid. Let's find some candy.'

Once he had kitted out the boy with sweets, a box of colour crayons and a soda pop, he looked up and down the street. 'Now let's get something for your ma. Think she'd like a new hat?'

'Last washday I heard her say she needed some new drawers.'

Hasty chuckled and mussed the boy's hair. 'We guys can't go sashaying into a store asking for feminine drawers! Next time we come to town I'll give her the money and she can buy some of those for herself. I think today we'll settle for a hat.'

He found a store and asked what was stylish. The proprietor took a large round box from a shelf. 'You're in luck, sir. Just in. All the rage back East.' He opened the box to reveal a flower-bedecked headpiece. He carefully extracted it and held it for inspection. 'See, it is wide-brimmed with slits at the sides. All the style.'

'What are the slits for?' Hasty asked.

'The lady threads a scarf through them and ties it in a pretty bow at her throat. Believe me, it's the latest thing.'

'What will they think of next?' Hasty exclaimed with a smile. But the smile disappeared when the man disclosed the price. Something unexpected must have happened to prices while he'd been inside. He gulped again when the fellow added, 'Of course, she'll need a real pretty scarf to go with it.'

Of course, Hasty thought, and that's not gonna come cheap either.

'Something really stylish,' the man continued. 'You're in luck. We've got new ones just in from Cheyenne.'

'You surprise me,' Hasty said. Not strong in the irony department, the man looked blank, an expression that evaporated when his customer confirmed his purchase and asked for them to be wrapped.

Back on the boardwalk Hasty looked at the hole in his billfold and consoled himself by the thought that his dear Charley was worth it.

He bought his other bits and pieces, got back in the wagon and flapped the reins, anxious to get out of a place that no longer had a welcome for him.

Come Sunday, the Jones family dressed in their best – Charley in her new hat – and took the wagon into town. As they passed the boardwalks he was once again aware of folks pointing and whispering. But no one spoke directly to them.

As they entered the church, a couple nodded when they couldn't avoid his glance, but again none ventured a spoken greeting. It was the same after the service.

When they were leaving only the preacher acknowledged his presence. 'Good to see you back in the bosom of your family, Mr Jones,' he said, giving a slight nod before directing his attention to the next family in the line.

'I suppose that's a start,' Charley whispered as they strolled back to the wagon.

'Start, my eye,' Hasty said, setting his hat back on his head. 'He only spoke because he couldn't get out of it.'

Back home, Charlotte changed into her house-clothes, donned her apron and began bustling round the kitchen fixing Sunday lunch.

Hasty sat at the table staring at the surface of the tablecloth. 'Back there at the church, it was just the same as when I went to town the other day. Folks turn away. Hardly anybody says a howdy. And nobody's willing to pass the time of day with me.'

'It'll take time.'

'No, nobody's gonna forget.' He ruminated silently. Then, 'I feel I don't belong here anymore. I'm a foreigner anyways.'

She turned from her chores, a concerned look on her face. 'You feel you don't belong here – with me and Jimmy?'

'No, in this place – the town.' He turned and looked straight at her. 'What would you say about us pulling up our picket pin and settling someplace else, Texas say?'

'We can't up sticks, Fred. We're in our thirties now. What little we got is sunk here. Whatever money we could get for it wouldn't be enough to travel and start all over again. Facts are facts. At our time of life, this place is *all* we're gonna get, dirt floor parlour and all. It's up to us to make the best of it. We've got a roof that don't leak, we grow our own food. Sell a little surplus to earn a few dollars. There's a warm bed for Jimmy.'

He nodded. 'True. And I thought maybe I could pick up where I left off. Lord knows, there's enough catching up for me to do about the place. But since I been back, I been thinking. A community is about decency and neighbourliness with nobody stepping on any toes. I ain't just stepped on toes, Charley, I killed the local sheriff. And for no reason. That's just short of killing the local preacher. Ain't nobody gonna forget that.'

# EIGHT

The next day, after a morning working on fences, he returned to the house passing a line full of drying clothes. He washed up at the trough in the yard and settled down to lunch. They were part way through their meal when Charley looked up from her plate. 'Oh, by the way, there's a letter in the kitchen,' she said. 'I was clearing out your pockets in preparation to clean your jacket earlier this morning and that was in it.'

He went to the kitchen and returned with an envelope. 'Yeah,' he said, when he'd opened it. 'Came to the prison a week or so before I left. Plumb forgot about it, what with leaving and all.' He glanced at it and passed it to his wife.

'See me when you come out,' she read. 'Signed J. Kerr.'

'Yeah,' he said. 'That'd be Jacob Kerr, known as Jake.'

'What's it all about?'

'Dunno.'

'And who's this Jacob Kerr?'

'Jake Kerr, one of the punchers working for the Cruz when I was with the outfit. But don't really know him and haven't seen him for years. I'd recognize his face, but that's all. I have to go into town for supplies tomorrow. I'll check it out then.'

Tuscon still simmered with a latent hostility to the newly freed man. He tethered his horse at the end of town and strolled down the Calle Real, eventually pushing through the batwings of the Ocotillo Saloon.

The barman looked up as he wiped the bar. 'So they finally let you out.'

'Yeah. Got back last week.'

The man continued eying him, no invitation in his face.

'Listen,' Hasty said, breaking the awkward silence, 'I'm looking for Jake Kerr. You seen him? Know where he's at?'

The barman waved his hand around the scene. 'This place changed much while you been away?'

Hasty glanced around, not understanding, and offered a quizzical, 'No.'

'Exactly. It's a saloon, not some danged information agency. Now are you drinking or not?'

Hasty shrugged and left. He tried several more saloons, some knew Jake Kerr, some didn't, but none knew of his whereabouts. In his stroll down the main street Hasty deliberately avoided the San Pedro Saloon – that was where it had all happened and it would bring back memories – but, turning up blanks, he finally resigned himself to checking the place out.

'Long time no see,' the barman said. There was a little more friendliness in his voice than the others, but not much. 'What you having?'

'Figure I owe you a drink, Pete,' Hasty said.

'What for?'

'If it hadn't have been for you it might have been the rope instead of manslaughter.' That was true. It had been Pete Lesley's testimony that had got it on the record that the death was the result of a fistfight and that Hasty Jones had said nothing in the run-up that showed any intent other than having a scrap.

'You don't owe me nothing, Hasty. All I did was tell the truth. But the fact is, you still killed a man, an officer of the law at that.'

That was true too.

'I'll have a whiskey,' Hasty said, dropping a coin on the bar.

'And some more,' the barman said, nodding at the coin. 'Prices have gone up while you been on vacation.'

Hasty asked about Jake Kerr as he passed over the extra money, but the barman shook his head. 'Ain't seen him for quite a spell.'

Hasty looked about the room, noted the cold looks directed at him, and drained the glass in one go. 'See you.'

He was just making his way back to his horse when someone caught his arm. 'Well, I'll be, if it ain't young Hasty!'

He turned to see a familiar face. And for a change, a face with a smile on it. 'Mel Adams!'

'The very same, pal. How long you been out?'

'A week or more.'

They shook hands and leant on the rail overlooking the street. 'You know,' Hasty said, after they had brought each up-to-date on their doings, 'yours is the first friendly voice I've heard since I got back.'

'How long we go back together?'

'A long ways.'

'You're dead right, my old pal. Huh, I remember you as a snot-nosed kid who had trouble telling one end of a hoss from another.'

Hasty chuckled, shaking his head at the recollection.

'So I can talk straight?'

'Of course you can.'

'You've always been knowed to have a temper. From the time you was a greenhorn you was known to be the one looking for trouble. Well, after the killing, you got a rep for a lot more – in truth, a piece of real dynamite with a short fuse. And the fact is, nobody wants to be close when it goes off again.'

'And you?'

'Hey, I know the signs, don't I? Besides, you've never done me no hurt.'

'You're a regular guy, Mel.'

'And you're a regular guy, I know that. But you've gotta face it. Once in your past you've been a double-barrelled jackass and you're gonna have to pay the price. OK you've paid your debt to society, as they quaintly put it – that's part of the price – but you're gonna have to keep paying the price. That's the way of folk. That is, until what you've done fades.'

'It ain't gonna fade, Mel. They say elephants have long memories – well, folks have long memories too.'

'I didn't say "disappear", Hasty. It'll never disappear, but it will fade, believe me. It'll take time and you've got to be patient.' He chuckled as a thought struck him. 'Hey, that's another quality that a jackass like you has got.'

'What you mean?'

'You ever seen a pack mule being loaded? He stands there and takes it. That's patience. And that's how you gotta be. Patient as a pack mule.'

Hasty didn't see the humour.

Mel joke-fisted his shoulder. 'Come on, pal, let's have a drink.'

'Things are sure changing,' Hasty said when they'd settled into a saloon. 'Huh – the bustle! Population looks like it's going through the roof. The railroad. Buildings springing up everywhere. Wood and brick buildings too. Another couple of years it'll be as big as Denver. Frisco even.'

'Those aren't the only things that's different. The Cruz is under new ownership.'

Hasty nodded. 'I heard that Old Ben Matthews had passed on. He was a straight guy, good man to work for. Talking of the Cruz, that reminds me. You remember Jake Kerr, one of the hands out there? You seen anything of him lately? He sent me a note to see him when I came out.'

'No. Figure he's still on the Cruz's books. But I ain't seen many of the guys since I got laid off.' He patted his leg. 'Had a bad fall, broke the leg, didn't set right. I can still ride OK, but ain't no way I can jump down and wrassle down a young steer for branding.'

'So, what do you do now for a dollar?'

'Swamping, odd jobs. I get by. Anyways, back to the Cruz. Dear old Ben was pegging out. Never was too healthy in his later years, what with the wheelchair and all. It'd be not long after you got sent away. Anyways, Doctor had told him he'd got something inside eating him away and he wouldn't see the season out. Now, you know he'd got three sons. They were all capable boys; they'd been born and raised in the outfit. They knew the ins and outs of the cattle business so there was no problem about them managing the outfit after he'd passed on. Only trouble was, they was always arguing amongst themselves.'

Hasty chuckled in remembrance. They were still in their teens when he saw them about the place. One or the other would always be sporting a black eye that one of his brothers had given him.

77

'Well,' Mel continued, 'they were aiming to split the spread into three independent parts on the old man's death. That way, they could run their separate businesses the way they wanted and wouldn't be butting heads all the time. Reasonable idea in the circumstances and there was no cause why it wouldn't work. But when Old Ben heard about it he blew his top. He'd built the Cruz from nothing and wanted it to stay intact. He'd got nothing against his lads, but he didn't want to close his eyes for the Big Sleep knowing his beloved outfit was going to be broken up after his death. So he filed it in his will for the place to be sold and the money to go to his boys. That way, he was doing right by them – they didn't lose out – and his life's work wouldn't be shattered.'

'Who did he sell it to?'

'That's the interesting thing. William S. Thacker. You remember him?'

'Sure do. Got an office in one of the side streets off the Calle Real. I got Charley to ask him to be my lawyer but he declined.'

'The very same. Attorney. But a real, genuine nobody. I figure you were lucky he didn't handle your case.'

Hasty took a drink. 'The Cruz Cattle Company? One of the biggest outfits in the whole of the Territory? Where did a shyster lawyer get the grub-stake to buy that?'

'I figure he was more of a wheeler-dealing busi-nessman than a lawyer. Seems he'd been buying up stretches of land on the quiet. Sold them to the railroad company when they were pushing their tracks this way.'

'Must have pulled in a fortune.'

'Yeah, that's how come he could buy the Cruz outright. And have some loose change over.'

Hasty emptied his glass and stared at the bottom. 'All that going on while I was doing nothing but wield a prison shovel.'

It was after midnight when they finally lurched back on to the street.

Hasty looked up at the moon. 'Jeez, I gotta get back. I plumb forgot about the time.'

Mel chuckled. 'No way you're going back tonight, pal. You'll fall asleep at the reins and end up in an arroyo. You're stopping the night at my place.'

'No, Mel, I gotta go. Charley and Jimmy, they're all alone.'

The other laughed. 'Hell, they been looking after themselves for three years. They can manage one night.'

'But, Charley'll get worried – and angry.'

'She might get worried. That can't be helped; the damage is done. But she won't get angry. You're forgetting, I know her almost as well as I know you. When you get back tomorrow you tell her how we met up today and she'll understand. She knows what you're going through and that letting off a bit of steam like this can only help.'

'You sure?'
'Yeah, now where you left your horse?'
'Danged if I know.'
And they staggered into the night.

# NINE

When he awoke the light hurt his eyes and his head was pounding. His demeanour was not helped by the hooting of the train in the nearby railroad depot.

'Progress!' he murmured, as he slung his feet to the floor. When his boots clunked on the bare boards, he realized he was still dressed. He held his head in his hands contemplating a serious question. Was the smell of the frying bacon coming from the next room something which he relished? Or was the smell about to cause him to vomit? A deep philosophical question to which he couldn't find an answer.

He took a chance and stood up, then staggered into the adjacent room.

Mel looked up from his cooking. 'Jeez, your face! Ain't seen a green that rich since the grass after last spring's rainfall.'

Hasty groaned.

Mel grinned. 'Your system ain't used to booze, is

all. It's being prevented from letting alcohol wash through your guts for three years that's done it. Don't worry, pal, you'll get used to it again.'

But Hasty wasn't listening. Proximity to the frying pan had solved his philosophical question and he lumbered to the door, just managing to clear the building before emptying his stomach over the ground. He spent minutes with his head under the pump.

'Listen, pal, ' Mel said, as his visitor eventually returned. 'I'll ride out with you. Help smooth things over. Besides, I ain't seen Charley for a spell.'

When they were in sight of the homestead Hasty pulled in. He dropped down and began plucking Mexican poppies. 'Might help,' he said, forcing a grin to the face that was now devoid of green, in fact devoid of any colour at all. When he had gathered a bunch he heaved his body back into the saddle.

But Mel had been right. Despite the state of her husband, all Charley showed was genuine gladness that he had returned safely.

After sharing a meal with them and jawing over a few cigarettes, Mel hit the trail. Then, apart from some simple chores, Hasty did little for the rest of the day.

Having lost a couple of days, Hasty was up early the next morning eager to get some solid work done. The corrals presented the major challenge. Some posts simply needed re-fixing but others had keeled over completely and longer poles were needed to be sunk in deeper holes. He was working on one of the awkward ones, delving deep with his shovel, when he heard the drum of hoofbeats. He looked up to see four horsemen approaching.

He paused in his task and leant on his spade, at first interested but not concerned. 'Howdy,' he said, wiping his brow as they reined in.

'Your name Hasty Jones?' The questioner wore a small derby hat and there was something a mite familiar about the squareness of his face but Hasty couldn't place it. 'That's what folks call me.'

'Take him, men.'

'Hey, what is this?' Hasty snapped, backing off and raising his shovel as the other three dismounted.

'You killed my brother and now you're gonna swing from this here rope.'

'Dunno what you're on about,' Hasty retorted. The self-control that he had largely kept in check for the last three years suddenly broke and he swung his shovel viciously at the men who were beginning to circle him.

'I'm Les Kerr,' the man explained. 'Jacob was my brother.'

Then Hasty realized why there was familiarity in the face before him. Jake had the same square features.

'Yeah, Jake's been gutshot,' the man went on, 'deader than a doornail. And it's all over town how you been on the prod for him.'

'Jake – shot?' Hasty queried, as the news sank in. Then: 'Sure, I was looking for him. *Looking* for him. But not on the prod. I had no cause to harm Jake. He was an old pal of mine. You're putting two and two together and making five.'

'Wouldn't expect you to say anything less,' the man growled. 'Ain't never heard of a no-good admitting to anything yet.'

'He'd sent a note to me in prison,' Hasty said, keeping his eyes on the men circling him. 'Said he wanted to see me when I came out.'

'So you say,' Kerr snarled.

'If there's some suspicion,' Hasty yelled, 'I've got a legal right to state my defence to the proper authorities.'

'When you killed Jake you gave up your legal rights. And to hell with the proper authorities, anyhows. When you killed that other guy, they let you off the rope. We're just gonna make sure this time.'

At that point one of the man managed to grab Hasty and heave him to the ground, affording the opportunity for the others to leap on him. The shovel was wrenched from his grip and one smacked his head with a gun butt. When he recovered from the daze his arms were bound behind him.

He writhed and twisted. But it was in vain. He looked up to see Kerr taking a coil of rope from his saddlehorn.

The man looked at the cottonwood from which

hung the swing that Hasty had put up for Jimmy years ago. 'A convenient hangtree.'

The noose was put round his neck while two men held him and the other end of the rope was thrown over a sturdy branch of the tree. With arms pinioned and the noose yanked taut around his neck, resistance was impossible and the men had no difficulty hoisting him on to a horse.

'Hasty!' It was Charley screaming as she came running from the house. 'What's going on?'

'Stay back, Charley,' Hasty called. 'Keep out of it.'

'That's right, ma'am,' Kerr said. 'If you know what's good for you, you'll do as your husband says.'

One of the men grabbed Charley's arms.

'Ma! Pa!' This shout came from Jimmy, running from the fields where he had been playing. His cries mixed with his mother's screaming.

'And keep that kid back,' Kerr snapped at Charley, 'if you know what's good for him.'

Jimmy ran to his mother who clasped him to her side with her free hand.

Kerr nosed his horse nearer to Hasty and dismounted. 'Stand aside, men. I want the pleasure of slapping the bronc myself.'

'You got this all wrong,' Hasty managed to wheeze through his constricted larynx. 'I ain't killed your brother.' But his voice could hardly be heard above the screams of his wife.

'Time for talking's over,' Kerr growled, removing one of the gloves tucked in his belt, and flexing it in preparation to strike the horse's rear.

'You'd do this in front of my wife and kid?' Hasty croaked. 'At least get them out of the way.'

'Ain't got no time for niceties,' Kerr grunted. And he whacked the horse's rump.

The horse sped forward and Hasty caromed backwards out of the saddle, swinging to and fro from the branch.

To the screaming Charley it seemed like an eternity. But it was only a second.

There was a rifle crack. The split rope remained taut for a moment, then parted under the weight, dumping Hasty on the ground. Another shell gouted dirt up at Kerr's feet.

The four men whirled round, eyes raking for the source, finally seeing a figure half-hidden behind the corner of the house.

'This is a seven-shot Spencer,' the stranger called across. 'Enough to down all of you. And you've already seen enough to know how accurate I can be with it. Now vamoose.'

'Who the hell are you?' Kerr snarled.

The man fired again and Kerr's hat flew off.

'Somebody who's gonna put the next cartridge through your gut,' the stranger yelled, 'if you say just *one* more word and don't get your vigilante scum out of here.'

Scowling, the four men claimed their horses and headed out, with Kerr yelling, 'This ain't the end, Jones.'

Charley ran to her husband and worked feverishly to loosen the noose round his neck. The interloper joined her, while maintaining watch on the disappearing riders, his gun at the ready.

'Thank you, mister,' Charley said, as she examined Hasty's throat after she had removed the rope from his neck. 'Who are you?'

Hasty managed a smile, then croaked, 'Charley, meet Eight-Ball.'

# TEN

They were sitting on the porch drinking lemonade. 'That was real lucky you turned up,' Hasty said, feeling his neck. 'Couldn't believe it when I heard your voice.'

'Luck!' Eight-Ball endorsed. 'Sure was. Luck – that's a currency you and I ain't had too much of in recent times.'

Hasty nodded. 'Yeah.'

Eight-Ball gulped down some of the cool liquid. 'Saw some kind of commotion when I was riding up so worked my way round to the back of your house to get a closer look. What was it all about?'

'You remember that letter I got back in the pen? From an old workmate, Jake Kerr?'

'Yeah, asking you to see him when you got out.'

'That's right. So, not long after my return I went round town asking for him. But couldn't turn him up. Thought no more about it until his brother showed up just now with his sidekicks, saying Jake had been killed and he pegged me for it. The rest you know.'

'Yeah, organizing his own neck-tie party.' He paused, then, 'This Les Kerr and his entourage, you know where they hang out?'

'No.'

'Well, they're not regular cowpunchers. Not wearing derby hats and caps like that. Ragged denims and all. Could be homesteaders but I noticed one had chip hammers in his belt. I figure they're miners. It'd help if we knew where they hailed from. You know the mines hereabouts?'

Hasty shook his head. 'There must be a dozen mines in Pima County alone.'

'Anyways, listen, you're gonna have to tell the sheriff about this caper.'

'Yeah, I suppose so,' Hasty said, his fingers still tenderly exploring his neck again. Then, 'Anyways, what brings you out this way? Last I heard you were heading for California.'

'I was but changed my mind. Huh, can you imagine your old buddy Eight-Ball picking oranges? So I decided I'd look up a cousin Texas way. He's got a spread over in Los Cruces. As your place is on the way, thought I'd drop by, say howdy and lay my eyes on this beautiful wife you been telling me about for three years.' He glanced at Charley and winked. 'And he wasn't exaggerating about being a looker, ma'am, if I may say so.' He finished his drink, adding, 'And that explains the luck of me turning up.'

He placed the empty glass on the boards and looked out in the direction in which the Kerr mob had ridden. 'Listen, I'm staying over a spell with you.'

'Of course you are,' Charley said.

'Our house is your house,' Hasty added. 'You know that.'

'Thanks for the offer, folks – but whether you offered or not, I'd have invited myself! Before this matter with crazy man Kerr and his mob gets sorted out, we gotta be prepared for trouble. I figure that was no idle threat he was making about this not being the end of matters. So we gotta work on the assumption that they'll be back. And you're gonna need some back-up.' He gestured to Hasty's waist. 'You don't carry a gun, do you?'

'No.'

'Well, now's the time to start. You gotta take basic precautions and carry a weapon. You got a pistol and holster?'

'There's my father's old gun and rig packed away in a chest somewhere. He was a drover.'

'Well, wipe the dust off it and check it's working. Drovers' irons take a lotta knocks out on the range and ain't necessarily reliable.' He thumbed to the building behind him. 'And you're gonna need two guns in the house. One that you can get at quick and one out of sight that Charley can use if necessary.'

They went inside and Hasty nodded at the carbine in a rack near the door. 'There's one.' Then he spent some minutes rummaging through chests and eventually extracted a bundle. He unwrapped it to reveal his father's old weaponry.

Eight-Ball took the gun and examined it. 'Joslyn .44. Single action, side hammer.' He glanced at the chamber 'Five shot.' Then, hefted it. 'A little light.'

'All Pa needed it for was to keep cattle in order,' Hasty explained. 'Figure he probably never got through a chamber of shells in the whole of his working life.'

'Well, get that belt around your hips and we'll see if it still works.'

Charley set about preparing a meal while the two men went outside. Some minutes later a couple of bangs made her jump; but, with satisfaction, she realized the noise was telling her the old gun was still serviceable.

Later that evening they were seated around the table, having just finished supper. 'Any idea what this Jake Kerr wanted to see you about?' Eight-Ball questioned.

Hasty shook his head. 'No.'

Eight-Ball drew on his cigarette contemplatively and watched the smoke rise. 'Wonder if there's any connection between his wanting to see you and his getting bumped off.'

Hasty grimaced quizzically. 'Such as?'

'There's several possibilities. For instance, somebody might not have wanted him to speak to you.'

'Can't see anything he would have to say that

would be that important.'

'Or, somebody's got a grudge against you and, when they heard you asking after him, decided they could use the opportunity of knocking him off so that they could pin his murder on you. If they knew how impulsive his brother Les is, they could then let matters take their course. You know anybody who's got a grudge?'

'Well, my dear Eight-Ball, you know what I was in the pen for. I did kill somebody three years ago. Sheriff Syson. He's got family and friends. Judging by the ruckus folks were kicking up at the time, I figured none of them saw a mere four-year stretch as fitting punishment. Maybe there's still one amongst them who won't be happy until they see me on the end of a rope.'

Eight-Ball nodded. 'Could be. Wouldn't be the first time somebody's aimed to exert their own punishment on an ex-con.'

Charley dropped her head in her hands. 'After all we've been through,' she whimpered, 'I thought we'd paid the price, seen the last of it. But all this talk of guns and people wanting you dead, maybe we should move out like you said.'

Hasty clutched her hand. 'I been thinking about what you said, Charley, and you were right. We ain't got much but what we have got is all here.'

Eight-Ball stubbed out his cigarette. 'Don't know about that. That's a domestic matter for you folks to work out, but I figure the first thing you gotta do is tell the law what happened today. The law and I ain't never seen eye to eye, but they've got some usefulness and I reckon if you let them know what happened today, you've cleared the air. At least they'll know what's going on and with Les Kerr's name on their books it might make the critter think twice about his vigilantism.'

'I have to check in at the law office once a week,' Hasty said. 'I'll go in tomorrow and kill two birds with one stone.'

They rolled into Tucson the next morning. Rather than leave Charley unprotected back at the house they had decided to go in together. Hasty sat with his wife on the drive seat of their flatbed wagon while Jimmy sat at the back with his legs swinging over the tailgate. Eight-Ball accompanied them on horseback.

They parked the wagon while Hasty went to the law office alone, the others heading for the stores to get supplies.

'Didn't expect to see you again,' the sheriff said, when he saw his visitor come through the door. He looked at his deputy and rose.

'Why not?' Hasty asked.

'Toting a gun too, I see,' the lawman said as he moved clear of his desk. 'At least you've saved me a job.'

'How come?'

'I was just about to come out to your place.' Up till then the sheriff's voice had been low-key but suddenly his whole demeanour changed when both he and his deputy whipped out their guns and levelled them.

'Now let my deputy take your iron,' he snapped. 'Get it, Drew.'

Hasty stepped back, fists raised. 'What the hell's going on?' His words bore the keen edge of his sudden anger.

'Yeah,' the sheriff said, a hard smile coming to his tobacco stained lips. 'Go on. You let your temper take over, Jones, and you'll be gunned down where you stand. To tell you the truth, that'd suit me fine. Now do as you're bid, quiet like.'

For a few moments defiance glared out of Hasty's eyes. Then the logical part of his brain took over and he sought to control the fury that had welled up inside him. Eventually he unclenched his fists and raised his hands, allowing his gun to be removed. 'OK, what's going on, Sheriff?'

'Move your ass back to the jail.'

Hasty remained motionless for second, then moved in the indicated direction. 'I'm doing as you say 'cos I'm looking down two gun barrels, not 'cos I know your reasoning.'

# ELEVEN

'The reasoning is,' the sheriff said, once Hasty was behind locked bars, 'you've been home less than a week and there's been another killing in my bailiwick.'

'If you're talking about Jake Kerr, then I know.'

'You bet your ass you do.'

The prisoner grabbed the iron rods of the cage. 'Listen, Sheriff, that's the reason why I'm here, in your office. To tell you that his brother and his gang tried to lynch me yesterday. Out there, at my own place, in front of my wife and kid.'

'They did? Pity they weren't successful.'

Hasty rammed his face between the bars. 'You bastard.'

The sheriff smiled, knowingly. 'Ever since I knowed you, Jones, you been on a path of self-destruction. Only it ain't straight; it kinda arcs round. That's why you can't see it. But you're heading straight for Hell. Only a matter of time.'

'But they got this thing all wrong, Sheriff. Like you have.'

'Yeah. You, a convicted murderer with a hell-bent crazy nature, are asking after Jake. Next thing he's been gunned down.'

Hasty clenched the bars harder, turning his knuckles white. 'I ain't denying I was asking after him. But I didn't find him, and I sure didn't kill him.'

The sheriff leant against the wall opposite. 'Why were you asking after him?'

'When I was in prison he sent me a note for me to see him when I came out.'

'What did it say?'

'Just to contact him.'

'If that's the case, why did you wait? You'd been back some days before you started asking after him.'

'Yeah. I'd forgotten about it. Hell, it's been a big thing, coming back after three years, Sheriff. The note skipped my mind temporarily, is all. My wife found the note in my jacket when she was getting it ready for the wash.'

The lawman chewed on his tobacco, saying nothing, so Hasty added, 'Anyways, if I was aiming to kill him, would I let everybody know I was looking for him?'

The sheriff leant over and sent a stream of juice into the spittoon in the corner. 'Huh, who knows how the hell your mind works. You got a crazy temper, always looking for trouble, everybody knows that too.'

'And, if I'd done it, would I come waltzing into the law office? Listen, the reason why I came in to see you is like I said. Jake's brother came out to my place with a gang yesterday and tried to lynch me. Pegged me as Jake's killer 'cos I'd been asking after him. Just like you're doing.'

The sheriff stepped in the direction of his office. 'Where are you going?' Hasty shouted.

'To find the form and fill out the official charge.'

'I told you I didn't do it.'

'If the judge turns up, he'll be holding session tomorrow morning, and you can tell your tale of woe to him.'

Hasty realized he was up against a brick wall. 'In that case, get me an attorney.'

The sheriff laughed. 'You're out of luck. The shyster who got your last killing reduced to manslaughter has took down his shingle. Got himself a plum job in Territorial Capital.'

'I still got a right to an attorney.'

'OK,' the lawman said grudgingly. And Hasty heard him instruct his deputy to fetch a lawyer.

'And tell my wife,' Hasty added. 'She's shopping here in town. She's gonna be wondering what's happened to me.'

He sat down, thinking, and some ten minutes later he heard movement in the front office. Then he heard the sheriff asking, 'And who are you?'

'A friend of the family. Name of Tom Deeds.'

He heard Charley's voice. 'You stay here, Jimmy.'

Then the sheriff came through with Charley and Eight-Ball. The lawman looked at his watch and muttered, 'Ten minutes is all.'

The door clanked open and shut. Charley sat beside him on the bunk and gripped his hand. 'Oh, Fred, it's a nightmare. It's happening all over again.'

'No. This time I didn't kill anybody.'

'Any ideas on proving it?' Eight-Ball asked.

'How the hell do I do that?'

'You've been with me for most of the time since you came out,' Charley said. 'I'm your alibi.'

'From what I know of the law,' Hasty grunted, 'a wife's testimony don't count.'

Eight-Ball could see the angry frustration in his friend's face. 'Be patient, pal. All is not lost.' He went to the bars. 'Sheriff, when was this Jake Kerr feller killed?'

'Three nights ago.'

'That'd be Monday night.'

'Yeah.'

'What time?'

'The shot was heard about eleven.'

More concern crossed Charley's face and her hand shot to her mouth. 'Monday night! That was the night you didn't come home.' She burst into tears. 'Now I can't provide an alibi.'

'Even better,' Hasty said in a calmer voice. 'I was

with Mel Adams right through till the next day.'

'Who's this Mel Adams?' Eight-Ball asked.

'An old pal. We met up and drunk the night away.'

'Where can I find him?'

Hasty described where Mel lived, adding, 'Tells me he swamps out drinking parlours for a living. So if he ain't home try the saloons and cantinas.'


It was some two hours later that Eight-Ball returned with Mel Adams in tow. There were voices in the front, then the party moved to the cell.

'Where's Charley?' Hasty asked.

'I've settled Jimmy and his ma in a café,' Eight-Ball explained.

'So what have you got to say about all this, Mel?' the sheriff asked.

'Hasty couldn't have done it, Sheriff. He was with me all the time. We spent the evening drinking, then he stayed the night at my place.'

'I see,' the sheriff said. Them 'Hold on. Did he never leave you through all that time?'

'No.'

'I see. So you never slept?'

'Of course I had some shuteye.'

'Then how did you know he didn't slip out when you were sleeping?'

At that moment, there was noise in the front office and then the group was joined by an attorney. After he had introduced himself, the sheriff turned back to Mel. 'Like I was asking, how did you know he didn't slip out when you were asleep?'

'It was very late when we hit the sack. On top of that, we'd been hitting the liquor hard. He couldn't stand, never mind go out and fire a gun. Anyways, he wasn't armed.'

A reluctant concession was entering the lawman's eyes. 'You'd swear to that?'

'On a stack of Bibles.'

They looked at the attorney. 'He's got a good defence, Sheriff,' the man said. Murray grunted and unlocked the cell door. 'OK.'

Out on the boardwalk Hasty spoke to the attorney for the first time. 'Thanks for coming. Sorry you got inconvenienced when you weren't needed in the end. What's the bill?'

'Five dollars will cover it.'

Hasty passed over the amount and the lawyer touched his hat in acknowledgement.

'Five dollars for just crossing the road,' Hasty said, as the lawyer headed back to his office. 'We're in the wrong business.'

'Maybe you can get your five dollars' worth,' Eight-Ball said. 'You do have a use for the attorney. You're in the clear for the present, but these days anything can happen. I suggest we follow the attorney to his office and get him to take an affidavit from Mr Adams here attesting to all the pertinent facts. That way, should anything happen to him, you've still got an alibi that should stand up in court.'

The words brought a quizzical look to Adams's face. 'Anything happen to me? What you mean? Something like what happened to Jake?'

Eight-Ball smiled. 'Don't worry, Mr Adams. If these things are all connected, your providing an official witnessed statement will be an insurance for you as well.'

'How come?'

'That way, there'd be no point in knocking you off, would there?'

Adams still looked perturbed. 'I don't understand.'

'I'm not sure I understand a deal of what's going on around here,' Eight-Ball said, 'but come along all the same.'

As they came out of the attorney's office, dust was drifting in from the flats, wrapping the town in its yellow shroud. Eight-Ball coughed. 'I can't speak for you guys but I need something to wash this stuff out of my throat.'

'Good idea, pal,' Mel added. 'What with lawyers and affidavits, I need something to calm my nerves.'

Hasty nodded at the nearest cantina, handing a bill to Mel. 'The drinks are on me. I'll see you guys in there. First I need to let my missus know I'm out of the hoosegow.'

Relief showed in Charley's face as he relayed the news. 'And what about this Les Kerr?' she said, when he'd finished. 'He must be told.'

'Yeah, I'll get a note to him,' Hasty said. 'Meantimes, you be OK in here while I finish off a quick drink with the boys?'

'Of course.'

Over in the cantina he found his pals sitting in a corner. There were no more than half-a-dozen other people in the place.

'Talk of the devil,' Mel said, as Hasty dropped into a chair beside them, 'there's the new owner of the Triple C. Thacker. You remember him?'

In the gloom at the far end sat four men deep in conversation. Hasty didn't know Thacker personally but had vague recollections of seeing him about town years ago: a large, fat man with several chins and spectacles that gave him a schoolmasterly appearance. The man hadn't changed much as he remembered. Maybe another chin.

'Go on, introduce yourself,' Mel said. 'Won't do no harm to make yourself known. You know Old Ben said there was always a job for you with the outfit. Just in case you need work sometime, could be useful being in with the new guy. Like they say, another string to your bow.'

Hasty eyed the group. Alongside Thacker was a young bull-necked fellow with massive shoulders that swelled under a tight shirt. Another had a droop moustache and wore an army cap. The third was dressed in black leather with a pair of guns nestling on his hips.

'No thanks,' Hasty said. His mind wasn't really on

the matter. He was thinking of Charley and Jimmy still waiting in the café. 'I don't know about Thacker,' he added, simply to make conversation, 'but I don't care for the company he keeps. Especially the one with all the hardware.'

'That's Grant,' Mel explained. 'They say Thacker's got him on the payroll to handle any rustlers who try muscling in.'

'Hear that?' Hasty said, raising his eyebrows in mock concern and throwing a meaningful glance at Eight-Ball. 'They shoot rustlers round here.'

'Thanks for the warning,' Eight-Ball said, reciprocating the mock seriousness.

'I think they call the big guy Caspar,' Mel went on. 'And the fellow in the army cap goes by the name of The Major.' He sipped his drink. 'But I guess you might be right in your assessment, Hasty old pard. From what I hear, they're all on the unsavoury side of unsavoury.'

The three pals bantered for a while; but Hasty was set on getting back to Charley, which is why it completely slipped his mind about getting in touch with Les Kerr.

He swallowed the rest of his drink. 'Come on, Eight-Ball. Time to hit the trail.'

'Jeez,' he said when they finally drew up outside the homestead. 'I plumb forgot to get a note to Les Kerr to tell him I'm in the clear. I was aiming to do it while we were in town but I was so glad to get outa the hoosegow it got crowded out of my mind.'

'Yeah, I should have thought of that too,' Eight-Ball said. 'No never-mind. We'll just have to go back to town tomorrow, is all.'

# TWELVE

The next day was Jimmy's school day so, when he had been picked up, the three adults returned once more to town. Once they'd parked the wagon the two men left Charley to her own devices – she always relished a chance to visit the shops – while they headed for the post office.

'You know where Les Kerr lives?' Hasty asked the postmaster.

The man pondered. 'Last I heard he was working for the Bat Roost Mine. Figure he shacks up at the bunkhouse they got out there.'

Hasty penned a note addressed to Les Kerr. I'M REAL SORRY ABOUT YOUR BROTHER BUT CHECK WITH SHERIFF MURRAY. HE'S GOT PROOF I DIDN'T DO IT.

The two men were walking down the street back to the wagon when they heard squawks above the gabble of men's voices coming from behind one of the adobe saloons.

'Hey, ain't seen a main in a coon's age,' Eight-Ball said. 'Come on, pal. You and me need some light relief.'

They turned down the alley and shouldered through the crowd to see a wooden enclosure, waist-high. On one side stood a Mexican holding a shiny, feathered rooster tightly while the other an Anglo was holding a similar bird.

Around them, Mexican and Anglos alike were assessing the birds while eager hands took the bets.

'Come on, farm boy,' Eight-Ball said, 'give me the benefit of your experience. Which rooster should the big money go on?'

'Stop ribbing me, Eight-Ball. Don't know nothing about fighting cocks. The only thing I now about chickens is which one's a good layer.'

His companion assessed the birds. 'Well, I fancy the Mex's. It's a tad smaller and ain't squawking as much, but it's got a real mean look in its eye. Come on get your money out.'

'OK, I'll bet on the other critter. That way one of us comes out on top.' He eyed the bills Eight-Ball had pulled out of his pocket and was counting. 'But I'm only chancing a dollar.'

'I was right,' his companion said when they had placed their bets. 'The little un's the outsider, odds are higher.'

Some minutes later, when no one else could be encouraged to part with their money, the two birds were flung into the enclosure. With no preliminaries the creatures flew at each other bringing a roar from the crowd.

Rammed up against the enclosure the two visitors had a ringside view and within seconds Hasty was spattered with spotlets of blood. Not really interested, he pushed his way back, stepped clear of the throng and dabbed away the blood with his bandanna.

'Señor Jones?'

He stuffed the soiled cloth into his jacket and turned to see a Mexican in serape and sandals at his side. The man was leaning slightly towards him while feigning interest in the arena.

'Yeah?'

'Can we speak somewhere quiet, *señor*?'

'What's it about?'

'I mustn't be seen talking to you, *señor*. I'll walk to the next alley. Then you follow me.'

Hasty nodded back to the milling throng. 'I got a pardner here.'

'The matter won't take long, *señor*, and I think you'll find it's important.'

Before Hasty could put any more questions, the man was shuffling off. The young Texan pondered. Should he follow? Was it some kind of trick? He glanced at the roaring crowd around the main. Eight-Ball was lost in there somewhere, screaming his head off like the rest of the spectators.

He looked back and noted the man slip into the alley. Then, with one more glance at the noisy mass, he followed warily. Level with the alley, but keeping his distance, he looked into the narrow passage. Scattered about were rows of overflowing trashbins. The Mexican had dropped to the ground, back against the wall in between a couple of bins, and pulled his sombrero over his face, like he was taking a siesta.

Should be safe, Hasty thought, there was no one else. He joined the man, not too close and leant against the wall. He took out the makings and placed a foot on the bin next to the fellow in readiness to kick it at him should the need arise. 'OK, Pedro, what you got to say?'

'Jake Kerr was killed because he wanted to tell you something.'

'What the hell are you talking about? What could he want to tell me?'

'That you were framed for the killing of Sheriff Syson.'

'Framed?' Hasty grunted. 'I killed him. I know that much. I was there! I did it out of temper, but I did it.'

'That's what they wanted you to think, *señor*. And what they wanted everybody else to think.'

The memory of the incident came back as vividly as though it was just happening, the way it had played through his skull repeatedly for three years back in the sweltering heat of the pen. But this time, the scenario spun through his brain in seconds . . . busting through the door of the San Pedro; smashing the sheriff, jumping on him outside; and pummelling him senseless.

His mind came back to the present and he looked down at the Mexican. 'So what are you saying really happened that night?'

'The sheriff was on to Thacker,' the man said, 'so Thacker wanted him out of the way. He was in town with a couple of his boys that night. Hearing the ruckus they were watching your scrap from the other side of the street. When the two of you went down, both lying still, they crossed over to investigate. They realized you were out cold and Thacker saw his opportunity. One of his men, Caspar, twisted the sheriff's neck, broke it. If you have seen Caspar you'll know he's some big *hombre, señor*. Could break a bull's neck if he tried. Then they made themselves scarce.'

Hasty's mind was in a whirl. How could somebody else kill a man that he was sure he himself had killed? Was this true? Had he grovelled in a cramped prison cell for three years for somebody else's crime?

'Thacker was pleased with the night's work,' the Mexican continued. 'He'd killed two birds, as they say. He'd got Señor Syson out of the way and landed you with the blame.'

His voice trailed away and after a spell, he looked up fearfully at his silent listener.

'How do you know this is true?' Hasty asked. 'Were you there?'

'No, *señor*. No one knew of these things. Thacker and his men kept quiet about it. Nobody would ever have known but, some time after your trial, the Caspar *hombre* was drunk one night and bragged about it. I don't know if the story ever got back to town, but it's common knowledge amongst the regular hands out at the Triple C.'

The Mexican looked even more fearful. The bitterness swelling up in Hasty's heart was glowing in his eyes. If these things were true this man had kept quiet about them. He fought the impulse to lean down, yank the man to his feet and beat the living crud out of him. After a moment he said, 'Hell, why didn't you come forward before? You could have saved me three years living like an animal.'

The man shrugged and looked down at his boots. 'I know what you are thinking. *Sí, sí*, I feel like a rat, *señor*, but you don't know that Thacker *hombre*. Anybody gets in the way, he swats 'em like a fly. Leastways, he gets one of his hardcases like Caspar to do the swatting, but the result's the same. He made a stiff out of Sheriff Syson. And now Señor Jake is under the caliche. This Thacker is a clever, evil man. Uses his brain to make others do the work he won't do himself. We ordinary peons may know such things, but we are not all heroes.'

'So, if this stuff is true, why have you come forward now?'

'Jake Kerr was a good man, *señor*. I worked with him. He looked after my ass. Didn't treat me like greaser scum the way many gringos do.'

Hasty thought on it. Something didn't sit right, needed explaining. 'What do you mean – the sheriff was on to Thacker? What had Thacker got to hide?'

'You not know, *señor*?'

'No, that's why I'm asking.'

'Señor Thacker – he is a crook, *señor*. The *hombres* he's got around him – Caspar, The Major and the rest – they are what they call long riders. Thacker got to know them in his job as attorney. You are not a stranger to these parts, *señor*. You know that Tuscon is a haven for *bandidos*. It is not difficult to get such men around you. These *hombres* – he plans robberies for them out of the territory. Banks, mine payrolls. The law cannot chase them across territorial and state borders. Since he bought the Triple C his men can lie low in safety and wait until he's fixed up another robbery.'

'Doesn't make sense. With a spread like that he's a rich man.'

'No, *señor*. He doesn't know the cattle business. The company has been doing badly ever since he took over. Wasn't long before he got a passel of debtors' claims round his neck.'

Then Hasty recalled the rundown appearance of the place that he'd noticed on his homeward journey.

'The cattle business,' the man went on, 'she has just become a front for the activities which make the money.'

Hasty leant back against the wall in dumbfounded silence. 'What about the cowhands? Do they know about his shady doings?'

'Some do, some don't. He's only kept on a few

genuine ones, just for appearances. But they play deaf and dumb. Nothing to do with them is the attitude. Why should they do anything? They get a paypacket.' He rose. 'I must go, *señor*. I've risked myself too much as it is.' He glanced furtively up and down the alley. 'I pray to the Holy Mother nobody has seen the two of us talking together.' With that he pulled his sombrero low over his face again and scuttled down the passage.

Hasty leant against the wall, his brain still absorbing the information. Was such a thing possible? Was the man spinning a yarn? But why would he have told lies? On the other hand, the Mexican had looked genuinely scared as he had imparted the details. Eventually Hasty pulled himself together and tramped like a zombie to rejoin his comrade.

Back at the scene, it was clear the cockfight was over. The spectators had left the pen and were gabbling and gesticulating over the outcome. The smaller bird must have won because there was a man paying out and swearing.

'You were right,' Hasty said to Eight-Ball, ignoring the jubilation on his companion's face and the wad of bills he was waving. 'That business about Jake getting killed was to do with his looking for me.'

As Hasty began to relate what he had learned, the pleasure of winning evaporated from his companion's face.

'I hate to mention the law again,' Eight-Ball said when the explanation was over, 'but the sooner the sheriff knows about this the better. Come on.'

# THIRTEEN

The sheriff and his deputy were playing rummy when the two entered.

'You again,' the lawman said, putting down his hand. He picked up a smouldering cigarette from the edge of the butt-scarred desk and took a drag. 'What is it this time?'

'I've found out what the business is all about,' Hasty said, and he related what the Mexican had told him.

'All very interesting,' the sheriff said at the conclusion, 'but what do you expect me to do about it?'

'For Christ's sake, I've spent three years for a murder I didn't commit.'

The sheriff stubbed out his cigarette and replaced it with a bite of chew tobacco. 'Listen, Jones, that was an open-and-shut case. I was in court, heard it all. You're a guy who has a tendency for getting crazy, hopped up mad and in one of your gunpowder tempers you went too far. This guff about somebody

114

sneaking about in the dark and killing the sheriff while you weren't looking is just pie in the sky.'

The sheriff was right about the temper, Hasty thought, because it was welling up again; but he held it in check. 'Well, if you're not interested in helping me to clear my name, what about Thacker? He's organizing regular robberies – and has instigated two murders in the process.'

'That's quite a catalogue, but what you've told me is all speculation. From what I can tell it sounds like a Mex with some kind of grudge against Thacker and the Triple C. Just looking to cause trouble is all. These greasers get pushed around then try stirring something. It's happened before. Besides, Thacker is just about the biggest man in the county. I can't go out there throwing accusatory questions at him.'

'I thought law was about justice,' Hasty said. 'Not who's got the most dollars behind him.'

The sheriff rearranged the tobacco in his mouth. 'You been in the can for three years and you still think that?'

'Anyways, who's this Mex?' the deputy put in. 'What's his name?'

Hasty shrugged. 'Didn't give it.'

'Where's he live?'

'Don't know that either.'

The deputy looked at his boss. 'You're right, boss. The whole thing's a non-starter.'

'So you're gonna do nothing,' Hasty concluded.

The sheriff sent a stream of juice into the spittoon

and picked up his cards. 'Nothing I can do. Now whose go was it?'

Hasty opened the door. 'Well, something's gotta be done. If you ain't interested, figure the next step is the Territorial Law Office up in Prescott.'

'Give 'em my regards,' the sheriff said, without looking up. 'And shut the door on your way out.'

Out on the boardwalk Eight-Ball dug a crumpled pack of cigarettes from his pocket. 'That guy just wants an easy life.'

'It won't be so easy for him when I get the Territorial law in.'

'No, that won't faze him. They won't blame him for not listening to an ex-con. Besides, all you got is the say-so of a Mex you don't know or can get hold of. Even if you trace him, he'll go shtum. And the man with the tin badge is not bothered about you telling Prescott. Your record's gonna be your problem trying to get other law authorities to give you credence too. Murray knows that.'

It was early evening, not quite dark enough for lamps to be lighted, when a rider pulled into the forecourt of the sprawling white adobe that was the main residence of the Tripe C spread. He tethered his horse and knocked.

Inside he was shown to the big front room where Thacker was seated with some of his men.

'Drew,' Thacker welcomed. 'Good to see you. Help yourself to a drink. What can I do for you?'

'Got some news you may want to hear about,' Deputy Clayton said as he poured a whiskey at the cabinet. 'But it's gonna cost you more than a shot of rye.'

'OK, go on.'

'Hasty Jones came into the office today with some crazy tale about you and your men killing Sheriff Syson three years ago.'

Thacker shrugged. 'Some crazy tale all right. Where did he drag that up from?'

'Some Mexican whispered something in his ear then disappeared.'

Thacker didn't look perturbed.

'But there's more,' the deputy continued. 'He's trying to tie you in with the killing of Jake Kerr. And he knows about your out-of-territory capers.'

'All from the same source?'

'Yeah.'

'Does Jones know the greaser's name or anything about him?'

'No. But Jones ain't alone. Got a sidekick, name of Eight-Ball.'

'And what's the sheriff doing about it?'

'Nothing as usual. But there still could be trouble. Jones said he was aiming to take the matter to the Territorial Law Office.'

Thacker nodded. 'He is, is he?' Then, 'Anything else?'

'No, that's all. Thought you'd like to know.'

'You did the right thing,' Thacker said, rising and

crossing to his safe. He opened it and withdrew a wad of bills. 'I think a hundred covers it,' he added, as he passed the money to the deputy's waiting hand. 'For telling me and, of course, for keeping your trap shut.' He crossed to the door and opened it for the man to leave. 'OK, thanks again; and keep me informed of any developments as usual.'

'I think it's time that Jones was snuffed,' Caspar said, as they heard the deputy's boots on the planking in the hall fade. 'Just say the word, boss.'

'No, it ain't that easy. We knock Jones off, there's still his missus and his sidekick to raise a stink.'

'We can put them out of the way, too.'

'Don't be stupid. Murray would sure have to do something then. Even though the feeling in town is against Jones, they're gonna get riled at the killing of a woman.'

'So how do we handle it?'

'We drive 'em out.' He smiled coldly. 'Then, once they're out of the county, beyond Murray's bailiwick and on some lonely trail – who knows? – anything can happen.'

# FOURTEEN

'I can't believe you're cleared of Sheriff Syson's killing,' Charley said as the foursome finally settled round the table for the evening meal. 'I've lived with the notion for so long. It's tremendous news. I still can't get over it.'

'I ain't cleared yet, honey,' Hasty said. 'It's still gotta be proved. And the evidence for me is flimsy. We've gotta track down that Mexican somehow.'

'I've told you,' Eight-Ball said, 'even if we can trace him, there's gonna be the problem of getting him to testify.'

Hasty nodded. 'OK, but what I'm banking on is that if he knows, I guess others know too. So he isn't my last chance.'

'First thing is to put some kind of case before the authorities.' Eight-Ball said. 'Any ideas on how you're gonna do that?'

'The thing is too big for a letter. I don't trust the

mail anyhows. It's gonna mean a journey out to Prescott. And I ain't leaving Charley and Jimmy, so we'll all have to go. The sooner the better – so I figure tomorrow. That OK with you folks?'

With the matter agreed they turned their attentions to the heaped-up plates. Each with their own thoughts they continued their meal without speaking. That is, until a couple of shots shattered the evening quiet.

Both men leapt from the table and proned themselves against the windows, guns in hand. 'Turn out the lights, Charley,' Hasty said.

When the place was in darkness they peered cautiously around the window jambs. Then another couple of shots.

However, there was no breaking glass or the sound of slugs into woodwork. 'Whoever it is,' Eight-Ball whispered, 'don't seem like they're shooting at the house.'

They waited in that fashion for a few minutes, the only sound being the ticking of the banjo-clock and the occasional crackle of burning wood in the stove. As their eyes adjusted to the darkness the two men exchanged questioning glances.

Hasty holstered his Joslyn and claimed the spare gun. Checking it, he passed it to Charley, then grabbed the Winchester. He cocked it and eased open the door.

'Don't chance it,' Eight-Ball said. 'The lull might just be they're waiting for a clear shot.'

Hasty ignored the warning. Once outside he slowly crouch-walked along the veranda.

Then he heard Eight-Ball call from inside, 'I'm going out by the back door.'

Hasty waited at the end of the planking, peering into the gloom. Eventually he could make out the shape of his companion edging along the side of the building. When he knew Eight-Ball was close enough to see him clearly, he indicated silently with a pointed finger that he was going to move away from the building. He got to the first corral without incident. By the time he got to the second, Eight-Ball was close again.

'Christ,' Hasty breathed. 'So that's what they were up too.' Through the murk he could make out the bulk of their two milk-cows; both grounded and unmoving.

'Jeez, the horses!' he gasped, and worked his way round the building. But as he approached he could hear faint nickering. There was no pain in the sound, just the tones of being disturbed. After he had verified there had been no violence against them, he loped back to Eight-Ball.

'Figure this is just a token,' his companion whispered. 'Aiming to scare you off.'

'Yeah, let's get back to the house.'

Guns at the ready they backed through the gloom. Suddenly unseen weapons exploded again, prompting both men to race to the door. Hasty was first to make it, then Eight-Ball fell through. Hasty slammed the door shut but the windows were being blasted to pieces around them and they all had to stay on the floor. Then, equally suddenly, it was just as quiet as before.

Charley was under the table trying to console the whimpering Jimmy. For a while Hasty listened to the silence, then inched across the floor to Eight-Ball. 'Well, if they're trying to scare us off, they're doing a darn good job.'

But all he could hear from his companion was troubled breathing. It was clear the man had been hit.

'Jesus,' Hasty muttered. The old anger fired through his being and he leapt to his feet, flinging open the door.

'Hasty!' Charley yelled. 'No!'

But he marched brazenly into the yard.

'Here I am,' he yelled, challenging the darkness with his Winchester, sweeping it left to right and back. 'I'm the one you want. Take me on, you bastards!'

But there was no reply. He turned his head, this way and that in search of sound. Eventually he could make out the sound of distant hoof-beats. He waited until they had completely faded, and returned inside.

'Charley, Jimmy, you all right?'

'Yes.'

He knelt beside his companion.

'Don't be concerned,' Eight-Ball said with a

chuckle. 'I don't think they've killed me.'

'Well, I figure they've gone,' Hasty said. 'Heard the sound of horses. Will you be OK for a while?'

'Yeah.'

Hasty returned to the door and looked into the night. 'OK, we'll leave it ten minutes to make sure, then light one of the lamps.'

At the appointed time, the light showed the interior to have the appearance of a battle zone.

With Charley holding a lamp close, Hasty inspected his companion's wound. 'Bullet scored across your side,' he concluded. 'Doesn't look too bad, but we're still getting you to the doctor.' He looked at his wife. 'And I'm getting you and Jimmy to town too. The critters have won. We can't live like this.'

In town, Eight-Ball was attended to. The layman's diagnosis had been right. Despite the blood, the wound was no more than a nasty slit across the surface.

'Nothing serious,' the doctor said. 'But it's gonna smart for a while.'

'Tell me something new,' the patient wheezed, wrinkling his eyes as medication was applied.

While the doctor set about the bandaging, Hasty left to fix accommodation. He found a place at the edge of town in the Mexican quarter and, once he had the three ensconced, he went to the law office, noting the light coming from the window denoting someone was in occupation.

But yet again he drew a blank. 'There's nothing I can do, Jones,' was the sheriff's conclusion. 'I can ride out to the place tomorrow like you suggest, but there's no way I can find out who did it.'

'I know who did it! It was Thacker and his Triple C bunch.'

'You keep saying that but did you see 'em?'

'No. There was just lots of shooting in the dark.'

'If you can't identify 'em, I have nothing to go on.'

Hasty left without comment. On his return he passed a crowd at the end of the street. They were looking out across the flats.

'Somebody out there is having one hell of a barbecue,' he heard someone say. He looked at the focus of the crowd's attention. There was a glow on the horizon. A hand clenched his guts into a ball. It was in the vicinity of the homestead!

He went to the livery where their wagon and horses were quartered. He was thankful that before leaving, he had thrown whatever items he could on the wagon, including a saddle.

Fixing up one of the horses, he rode out. The nearer he got, the more he fretted that it was his place going up in flames. Then his worst fears were confirmed. When he finally made it he could see the whole place was ablaze.

There was little he could do. He dismounted and circled the conflagration in the hope that he might be able to save some of the livestock but the heat was too much for him to get close.

He mounted up and returned to town, finally falling asleep with a whimpering Charley in his arms.

# FIFTEEN

At sun-up, he took out the wagon to see if there was anything he could salvage. The adobe shell of the house was still standing but fire-blackened, with smoke wisping up from the gutted interior.

He staggered, heavy-footed with despondency, around the remains of his property. The barn, like everything else of wood, had gone.

With a heavy heart he inspected the stock enclosures; saw the pitiful black frame of the goat, roasted alive, before her tethering had burnt through; the chickens, burnt to death, trapped in their coop.

At least the sty was empty, its wooden gate flattened. Made of adobe the enclosure would not have been susceptible to the fire; and the pigs must have smashed through the gate in their terror. Now the creatures would be fending for themselves out in the wilderness. Well, good luck to them.

He kicked aside the charred remains of the veranda planking and stepped up into the place that had been their home. Only a few metal items had survived the inferno. In the area that had been the kitchen, he came across blackened pots and pans amongst the ashy debris. He thought of retrieving them – then thought, hell, what's the point?

Back at their temporary quarters in town, there was only Eight-Ball. Laid out in his bed, there was concern in his eyes. 'Hasty,' he said, 'there's been an accident.'

'Charley?' Hasty gasped, aware of her absence since he had entered the place. 'Yes. Got run down by a wagon. She's over at the doc's.'

Before he could give any more explanation, Hasty had dashed outside. The doctor met him as he burst through the door.

'Don't worry,' the man said. 'She's badly shaken but otherwise OK. I've checked her over. There's a little bruising but nothing's broken.'

The doctor showed him through to a back room where he found a white-faced Charley in bed with Jimmy at her side.

'She was out cold when they brought her in,' the doctor added. 'But I figure she'd only fainted. However, she'll have to rest awhile. I've given her something to keep her awake. It's important she doesn't fall sleep until I'm sure there's no concussion.'

Dropping into a crouch at the bedside Hasty instinctively put an arm around his son as he asked,

'What happened, honey?'

'Don't know. One moment I was crossing the street and suddenly someone shouted and I saw these horses bearing down on us. Luckily Jimmy was ahead, but one of the horses caught me. Next thing I knew I was where you see me now.' She paused, noting the blackened hands of her husband and soot-smudged clothing. 'And what's happened to you?'

'Don't worry about me, honey,' he said. 'Ain't nothing that can't be washed off.'

The doctor put his hand on Hasty's shoulder. 'It's best if we leave her quiet for a spell. I suggest she stays here for an hour or so where I can keep an eye on her.'

Hasty bent down and kissed her forehead. 'Yes, you rest, honey. I'll clean up and come over later. Come on, Jimmy.'

Outside, there were a couple of Mexicans sitting on the edge of the boardwalk. Seeing Hasty, one stood up. 'I saw it all, *señor*.'

'You did? Tell me.'

'I was sitting on the boardwalk, just like now. And I saw a wagon with two *hombres* in the seat moving along the street. At first I though nothing of it, but it did look a little odd the way it was moving. You know, *señor*, the horses set at a very slow walking pace like they were going no place. But there was a funny look in the *hombres'* eyes. They were both staring ahead. Very hard, like so.' He squinted his eyes. 'Then suddenly the fellow with the lead reins slapped them hard and the wagon, she whoosh forward.'

He demonstrated the speed with a violent outflinging of his arm. 'And your woman, she get knocked down. Didn't look like no accident to me, *señor.*'

'You know the drivers?'

The man looked from side to side, and his voice lowered. '*Sí*, señor. They were *hombres* who work for Señor Thacker.'

'*Sí, señor,*' the other added. 'The ones called Caspar and The Major.'

Hasty tensed as, once again, the familiar anger erupted inside him. He grabbed Jimmy's hand and dragged him back to their quarters.

'Calm down,' Eight-Ball said, after Hasty had growled out through gritted teeth what he had learned. 'Ain't nothing to be gained by blowing a fuse.'

'Hell, they've burned down my place, shot my best pal, now they've tried to kill my missus.'

'Don't think it was their intention to kill her. They've got you out of your place, now they want to get you out of town. Turning on Charley like that was just a warning.'

'Ain't the point,' Hasty snorted as he paced up and down. 'They could have killed her.'

He stopped at the door, outstretched an arm, his hand on the doorjamb. He leant in that way staring intently at the floor as he chewed over the business.

'A spineless sheriff who'll do nothing. Well, something's gotta be done.'

And he stomped out the room.

# SIXTEEN

In the livery he rummaged through the contents of the wagon. The ostler, sensing unstoppable determination in the man's movement, watched him in silence. Hasty rooted out his Winchester and ammunition, then took his horse from the stall and saddled up. But, by the time he was tightening the cinch, some rationality was beginning to break through his anger and he paused in his actions.

He had to think things through. If he went riding out to the Triple C in broad daylight he wouldn't get within a mile of the place. He would sure as hell be spotted by Cruz outriders.

Wait till night? No, darkness would give him cover but would also hamper him. Besides he didn't have the patience to wait that long. So, how could he get out there in daylight without being seen?

He pondered on it. Hey, the stage did a mail-stop on the way in. That was it – the stage! The afternoon stage would probably stop with company mail too.

That would give him cover. What time did it leave? Two o'clock?

'What's the time?' he asked the ostler.

'Dunno. Figure getting on for two, I reckon.'

'Take care of the horse,' Hasty said and ran to the door. If only he were in time.

Dropping everything he dashed outside and belted down the street, relieved to see the coach and six mules standing near the depot. Jez, the stage driver, was leaning against a wheel, looking at his watch.

'Hi, Jez,' Hasty called breathlessly, 'got a favour to ask.'

'Hi, Hasty. Say, real sorry to hear about what happened to your place. A real rough deal.'

'I want to get out to the Cruz.'

The driver returned his watch to his vest pocket. 'No problem. We call there on the way out.'

'That's what I hoped. But there's a snag. I don't want to be seen. So I'd need dropping off some ways before.'

The driver looked in puzzlement at the man beside him, and for the first time saw the manic severity of his expression. 'Hell, I don't know about that, Hasty. I'm just a workaday stage-man. If there's trouble brewing with the Triple C, I don't want any part of it. I got a wife and kid to think of.'

Hasty felt like snapping, 'I got a wife and kid, too', but he held himself in check and said, 'Listen, Jez, if I ain't seen dropping off, you won't get into any trouble.'

The driver continued looking into the man's eyes. 'You and me, Hasty, we've knowed each other a long time. You know I only plain-talk yuh. I ain't got no clue what you're doin' but whatever it is, you sound like you're heading for a passel of grief.'

'Then, for old time's sake, don't make it difficult for me. And don't tell nobody.'

'Hell, what *are* you planning?'

'You not knowing is one of the ways you don't bring trouble on yourself. As far as you're concerned I'll just be a fare-paying passenger.'

The driver contemplated, then took out his watch again. 'OK, we pull out in five minutes. As to not being seen, you're in luck: there ain't no passengers booked on the outward trip.' He thought some more. 'There's a bunch of cottonwoods on the approach to the place. If you drop off there you shouldn't be seen.'

Back at the livery, Hasty wrenched the Winchester out its scabbard and stuffed ammunition in his pocket, telling the ostler to restall his horse. When he returned to the coach, Jez was already on the box, ribbons between his fingers, foot tapping impatiently on the brake.

'Judas Priest,' he breathed when he saw the Winchester in Hasty's hand. 'You're quite right – the less I know what's in that mind of yours, the better. Get yourself aboard, younker.'

Hasty took a seat and heard Jez kick off the brakes with a 'Yip! Yip!' The six mules started forward and the stage began to roll, rocking on its fore-and-aft springs.

Soon the vehicle was bouncing across the flat-lands, leaving a spume of dust in its wake. After half an hour, they turned off the regular trail and headed on to the Cruz spread.

'Keep your head down, younker,' Jez shouted. Hasty dropped to the floor, took off his hat and furtively peered over the ledge of the window. They were passing a couple of the outfit's men brewing up coffee at a makeshift bivouac near some cattle. The men waved, seeing nothing suspicious in the stage and its regular driver.

The further on to company land they travelled, the more crewmen they saw.

'Get ready, younker,' Jez suddenly shouted, above the crunch of metal rims and thud of hoofs. 'Cottonwoods coming up.'

Hasty peered out, noted the circumstances.

'Way over to the west, there's some more drovers,' the driver continued, as he slackened the ribbons a little. 'If you drop out on the blind side, keep low and head for cover they shouldn't see you.'

He slowed the vehicle some more. 'And don't leave the door open. It'll cause suspicion if I roll up to the place with a door flapping in the wind.'

Hasty leant the Winchester on the seat with its butt poking out of a window. He eased himself through another window and, gripping the overhead baggage rail, hauled himself through. Once he was clear,

134

holding onto the rail one-handedly with feet positioned on the outer ledge of the door bottom, he grabbed the rifle and pulled it out.

'Thanks, Jez,' he said, as he hung braced against the side, gauging the situation ahead.

The driver glanced down. 'Well, whatever you're up to, pal, good luck.' He slowed some more and Hasty leapt clear. He hit the ground at a roll and loped to cover as Jez flicked the ribbons on the lead mules for the coach to regain speed.

From behind the stand of trees Hasty watched the coach continue toward the main ranch house. Eventually, the stage lumbered to a stop outside the *casa principal*. Someone came to the door. There was an unheard exchange of words, then Jez flicked the ribbons and the stage began to roll once more.

Hasty waited for the man to return inside, then glanced around. No one else visible at the moment.

As he assessed the situation, the irrationality of his action for the first time began to nag at him. Here he was yet again, hasty by name and hasty by nature. Hell, he was no gun artist. And there was a bunch of hardcases ahead of him. What did he expect to achieve? Other than offering himself up to get gunned down – which would suit Thacker down to the ground. With one shot from one of his gunnies, the niggling fly in the ointment – Hasty Jones – would be out of the way.

But his brief reservations were dispelled when he thought of the way Charley had been ridden down and the three years – three irreplaceable years – that Thacker had taken away from him. And his blood returned to the boil.

Circling wide to minimize the chance of his being seen from the front of the building, he moved at a fast crouching run. Some yards from the complex he dropped behind a drinking trough.

He was eying the place, waiting for his chance when there was a noise to the side. One of the Mexican hands was coming out of a barn and heading straight for the trough. At a distance Hasty couldn't be seen – but up close there was no way he could remain undetected. As he neared, the man pushed his sombrero back, clearly in preparation to douse his sweating face. Surprise hit his features when he caught sight of the Winchester levelled at him.

'Come here,' Hasty hissed. 'Don't make any noise and nothing will happen to you.'

When the Mexican was up close, Hasty pulled the man's gun from its holster and dropped it into the trough. 'How many men in the *casa principal*?'

The man shrugged. 'Six, seven, eight. Who knows, *señor*?'

'*Gracias, amigo*. OK, now vamoose gentle-like and keep quiet. Make yourself scarce, that way you won't get hurt. This is nothing for you to get involved in.'

Hasty watched the man do as he was bid, walking on past a corral. When he was sure the man was no threat, he returned his attention to the building. Apart from an occasional faint, indistinct sound coming from inside he heard nothing save for the drone of insects.

The inactivity under a relentless sun made him irritable. His joints began to ache. Sweat trickled into his eyes. The gun became sticky in his hands.

Then the door opened again. He wiped the sweat from his eyes and but couldn't make out who it was. But whoever it was, he'd do for starters.

He lined up and pulled the trigger. The man slammed back and crumpled to the ground, jamming open the door.

There was shouting and doors began opening all over the place. Hasty painstakingly levered the Winchester and lined up again. Remaining hidden, somebody hauled in the groaning man. The shouting continued sporadically. Then a figure started to edge forward alongside the wall of the ranch house. Hasty smiled sardonically to himself. It was the man called Caspar. He couldn't have wished for a bigger target.

Caspar stopped at the corner, scanning the terrain, gun in hand. Hasty kept still. Waited. Then the man took furtive steps into the open. Hasty pulled the trigger a second time. The big man spun round and thudded to the ground. But the shot had pinpointed Hasty's position and resulted in a crackle of gunfire from the main building and bunkhouse. Hasty cowered behind the trough, taking the opportunity to lever his Winchester as bullets whined around. Chunks of wood gouted out of the trough causing water to jet from a myriad holes. After a deaf-ening minute the firing crackled to a silence.

'Who's out there?' Thacker's voice boomed. None of his men knew.

'Guess!' Hasty rejoined without breaking cover. Another crackle of shots. Silence. Then, Thacker again, 'Who is it? Any of you guys know?'

Hasty paused and thought on it. He wanted Thacker to know who it was. 'The man you sent to the slammer for three goddamn years,' he yelled.

He heard a buzz of voices.

'It's that pissant sod-buster,' someone shouted.

'He ain't gonna be no trouble,' another observed.

'Depends who he's got with him,' one commented loudly.

Then a coldness came over Hasty. He knew the chance of surprise had now gone and with it went the blind drive of unthinking emotion. He was becoming rational again. He could now view with some objec-tivity the situation into which he'd hot-headedly thrust himself. And he didn't like it. But he had no one to blame but himself. He'd spent three years learning to control his impulses and now he was back to square one, anger pounding inside him. There must have been other ways to get Thacker. More sensible ways.

Hell, no use crying over spilt liquor. He'd called the hand. Nothing for it but to make the best of a bad job. Like Eight-Ball said: you gotta have the sand to see things through. He had ammunition and weapons. He'd proved he had reasonable accuracy. Provided he could find good cover he could make it difficult for them. Even take one or two of the bastards before they got him. Yes, they'd get him eventually. It was just a matter of time. The gods were smiling on him – but not enough to prevent the inevitable.

# SEVENTEEN

He looked back. He'd have to move now they knew his position. God knows how many there were in there. If there had been eight like the Mexican was surmising, there were now six. That was enough to surround him in minutes and use him for target practice. He pondered on his situation. To his right beyond the corrals the terrain became rocky, giving some elevation. Maybe he could make it.

At a crouch he left the cover of the bullet-shattered trough, but by the time he had reached the corrals, the shells whining over his head told him he had been seen. He wove between the fences. The milling, neighing horses gave him some cover. Clearing the corrals, he loped across the flat and made the rocks. Clambering over some, scuttling between others, he made his way upwards.

He glanced back to see men from the *casa principal* now out in the open, advancing and firing at the same time. At their head was the black-leathered gunslinger Mel had identified as Grant. Ordinary cowhands were coming from barns while others were riding in, drawn from their tasks by the sound of gunfire.

A large fat figure remained in the cover of the doorway. It was Thacker shouting orders. 'Spread out. Surround the critter.'

There was a lull. Then Hasty heard, 'Well, what the hell you waiting fer?'

'That's Hasty Jones out there, Mr Thacker.' It was one of the regular hands.

'Damn you,' Thacker answered. 'Do as you're bid.'

Then, another voice. 'He's right, Mr Thacker. We ain't had no part in your killing afore and we ain't starting now.' A different voice added, 'Specially when it's shooting at a harmless sod-buster!'

Hasty's heart skipped a beat. If Thacker didn't get backup from his hands the situation was altered a mite. And Thacker wouldn't turn his gundogs on his own workers – there were too many.

Silence reigned again until Thacker yelled, 'I'll deal with you lot later.'

He shouted out a bunch of names – his gunslinging sidekicks – giving them directions for their angle of attack, finishing with, 'Grant, you come with me.'

With the knowledge there were reduced numbers against him Hasty braved a look-see. It brought a crackle of shells his way – but not before he drew a bead on a gunny. He triggered instinctively and the fellow spun in mid-air, his momentum taking him forward so he landed yards away.

The remaining men had disappeared from view, giving Hasty a chance to change his position yet again. He continued to make his slow way upwards. He squeezed through crevices, hauled his tiring frame up steep grades.

A bullet ricocheted off a rock near him. Maybe fresher than he, his attackers were gaining. He'd just worked himself into a niche when another slug slammed into rock above him. He crouched, shielding his head as he was spattered with granite chips. He couldn't go any further. He fixed himself into a sitting position within the niche. This was it – the last ditch.

He took his Joslyn, checked it was fully loaded and laid it at his side in readiness. Then he rested the rifle barrel on his knees. Below him he could hear scrapings against rock, feet on gravel. He dearly wished he could lean forward and see his adversaries. It was stomach-churning, just listening to them getting closer, hearing the crunch of their boots but not seeing them. And he didn't have the ability to aim quickly, nor was he nimble enough to withdraw from view when sighted. More bullets whined close.

'We know where you are, sod-buster!' It was Thacker's voice, much closer now. Hasty looked about him, assessing the situation. There were three vantage-points from which he could be taken. From rocks on either side, and from a butte towering before him. At any moment one of the Thacker men could slip into place and pick him off. He didn't know which one to line up on. Huh, one chance out of three.

He levelled his gun and lined up on the butte before him. The midday sun was heating things up. Insects buzzed, down below the windmill clanked, time dragged. Suddenly to his right, a gun exploded and he felt his left arm zip back. It was Thacker, sixgun blazing. Instinctively, Hasty swung the Winchester in Thacker's direction and slung his bloodied left arm over the barrel. He pulled the trigger and when the smoke had cleared Thacker had gone.

He didn't know whether the ranch-boss had been hit or not. But for the moment it didn't matter because the one known as The Major had made it to the butte right in front of him and was emptying a .45 in his direction. Hasty had no cover and in his contorted position he couldn't relever the Winchester. With bullets ricocheting off the rock behind him, he struggled to get his handgun.

But he had no need. There was an explosion and the army-capped Major juddered, stood transfixed like some statue, then plunged from the butte. Hasty heard the squelching thuds as the body hit crags on the way down.

He sat looking at the vacant space. Then he twisted to look about him. What the hell had happened? He got a grip on the handgun and waited, heard nothing. He pulled himself to his feet.

He could see nobody, and no more shots came his way.

Before allowing himself to be lulled into a false sense of security he reminded himself there was one unaccounted for. He looked at the wound he couldn't feel. Didn't look bad. With his handgun ready, he limped downwards. He came to a point where he had a view of the ranch house below. No signs of Thacker. No signs of anybody.

There was an arroyo cutting from the rocks and veering round to near the ranch house. That would make a good approach. He staggered down, noting the gunshot and crag-ripped carcass of The Major as he passed.

Although he was occasionally in view of the building, there was no firing at him. What was going on? Where was everybody?

Reaching the flat land he collapsed just before the arroyo, hauled himself to the edge and rolled into it. He lay panting on the sandy bottom. He waited till he'd caught his breath and pulled himself to his feet. He loped in the direction of the ranch house.

After fifty yards he stopped, his heart pounding. The pace was affecting him. Ahead the gully began to curve. He worked his way around the bend. Least he had some cover for a piece.

All stove up, his head was down as he trudged. That's why he didn't see the black-leathered figure waiting for him, as he turned a new bend. It was the one called Grant, standing at the arroyo's edge, gun raised, all set for the killing shot.

'Goin' some place, farm boy?'

Hasty dropped to the ground and frantically tried to line up his handgun.

But before he could effectively do so there was a boom and Grant pitched into the arroyo. Seconds later, another figure appeared. Eight-Ball! And a smoking Spencer carbine in his hands.

There was disbelief in Hasty's eyes. 'You!'

Eight-Ball grinned. 'Figured it was time to get my old pardner out of a spot – yet again!' He laid down his gun and helped up the wounded man. Hasty was breathing heavy but he managed a question. 'Was that you – killed the other feller up on the butte?'

Eight-Ball shook his head. 'No, that was Les Kerr. He ain't quite the bastard we thought he was.' He pointed away from the arroyo. Jake's brother and a couple of men could be seen in the distance coming away from the rock formation.

'Well, I'll be . . .' Hasty whispered.

Eight-Ball gave Hasty his shoulder. 'When you went missing, we didn't know where you'd gone. We pondered on the facts of the matter and knowing what a crazy headstrong galoot you can be, figured you'd come out here to sort things out, all on your ownsome. I couldn't let my crazy pardner handle it alone so I headed out to see what I could do.

'Then, as we rode in, we passed the bulk of the Thacker outfit, heading to town. Told us what was happening. Said that they'd quit. That reduced the odds.'

'I sure didn't expect any backup.'

Eight-Ball sat in the shade of the rocks, breathing heavily, the effects of his own earlier wound taking its toll. 'The way you act, pal, you need some kind of backup whatever you do.'

Suddenly, from afar, Les Kerr yelled, 'Look out, Hasty!'

Behind them close by, one of Thacker's downed men was hauling himself to his feet. Whoever's bullet had caught him, it had only been a grazing one. Despite the glazed look in his eyes he was sufficiently recovered to have assessed the situation and to be going for his gun. Neither man had the chance to recover discarded weapons and fire them.

One-handedly Hasty grabbed his own rifle by its barrel and swung it round. The weight of the stock made it a formidable weapon as it arced round. The man saw it coming but only had time to raise his arms in protection of his head, taking the full force on his forearms.

He fell to the ground, groaning. 'You broke my arm.'

'Ain't that a shame,' Hasty said, stepping back and making an appraisal of the bodies and fallen men. 'Hey, where's Thacker? He just dropped. I thought he'd taken a slug but I ain't seen his corpse.' He looked towards the ranch house. Nobody to be seen; the courtyard was empty.

He gestured to the man groaning in the dust. 'Watch him, Eight-Ball.'

With that he made to go down the remaining slope towards the house. But bullets began spanging chunks of granite behind him. He dropped to the ground. Then caught a glimpse of Thacker. He was taking cover behind Old Ben's mounting block in the courtyard.

Hasty wormed his way along the ground while Thacker fired non-stop. Then, hearing the hammer fall on an empty chamber, Hasty smiled and stood up.

'You wouldn't shoot an unarmed man?' Thacker whimpered.

Hasty gave him a hard, cold look. 'An unarmed man? What safeguard is that? You've had unarmed men killed. That's as good as doing it yourself.'

'Listen, kid, you've got me wrong. I've cut corners, yeah. You have to in business.' He nodded at the bodies. 'I gave employment to men I thought were ordinary, hard-working guys. My failing was, I didn't know what they were like underneath. By the time they were spinning their mayhem in my name, it was too late. You know, like an unstoppable train. I'm not responsible for wrongs they've perpetrated. Believe me.'

'The last time I heard a load of flapdoodle like that, it was coming out of the mouth of a snake-oil salesman. Fact is, that's what you are. A snake-oil drummer turned lawyer, turned crook rancher who'll stop at nothing.'

Thacker stepped back, licking his lips. 'Listen, I'm a wealthy man. I can redress you for any wrongs my men have done.'

'Right up to the crunch, still a talker.'

Thacker suddenly turned and raced for the house.

Hasty walked casually after him. As he entered the lobby a Mexican serving lady scurried past him, fear in her eyes. He paused and listened. The noise of clattering directed him through the building to an ornately carved door. He pushed it open. Thacker's study. The man was behind a desk frantically going through the drawers.

'Looking for ammunition?' Hasty said, leaning against the polished wood of the door.

Thacker paused in his search and looked up. 'I've told you I'm unarmed.'

Hasty aimed his gun at the ceiling, pulled the trigger, the action resulting in nothing more than a loud click. 'See, I'm out of ammo too.'

Then, as Thacker's fingers clawed amongst the bric-a-brac on the desk-top, Hasty began to load his gun. When he'd finished, he holstered it, ambled over to the desk and picked up Thacker's gun, which he proceeded to fill from his own belt.

The ranch-owner stopped his frenzied searching and looked at him quizzically. 'What you doing?'

Hasty didn't answer until he'd filled the gun and placed it back on the desk. 'I'm no gun artist. You know – you being a lawyer, me being a brush-popper

– I figure I'm no better with a gun than you are. As I see it, in the matter of gunhandling, we're equally matched.'

'Eh?'

Hasty nudged the weapon towards his adversary. 'There you are, what you want, a loaded gun.' He stepped back. 'Pick it up and lodge it in your belt. The rest is up to you.'

Thacker wiped the back of his hand across his mouth, looked at the gun, then back at the man. 'I'll go along with that.'

The ease with which he said it, and the hint of a smile on his lips told Hasty the gun would never reach the man's belt.

And he was right. Thacker leant forward slowly, but the second his hand was round the butt, he thumbed back the trigger and fired.

In anticipation, Hasty dove sideways, simultaneously drawing his gun and blasting. While Thacker's slug smashed into the wood of the door behind which his target had just been standing, Hasty's took Thacker in the chest. The man rocketed back, for a second slumped in his chair, then slowly slipped into an ungainly heap on the polished boards. Hasty rose and advanced, keeping his gun ready. When he had checked the still form, and verified it was permanently stilled, he returned outside.

Les Kerr, his miner friends behind him, greeted him on the veranda. 'Big day at the Cruz,' he grinned.

Hasty shook his head in disbelief. 'How come you arrived on the scene?'

Kerr took off his derby and wiped his forehead. 'Got your note. Rode in to town to check with the sheriff. When I'd confirmed you were in the clear about killing my brother Jake, I looked for you to give my apologies for the way I'd buffaloed you. How you apologize to somebody for trying to string 'em up, I don't know – but I had to say something, let you know the air was clear. Then your pal Eight-Ball here told me he guessed you were heading out here. Man, trying to take on the whole mob single-handed, that was real crazy, kid. Anyway, I figured you need all the help you could get. Besides I had my own score to settle with Thacker.'

Hasty nodded back to the house. 'He's in there. Or at least what's left of him. No need to concern yourself with him. Both our scores have been settled.'

Kerr returned his hat to his head. 'There's still the matter between you and me. So anything I can do to make amends, kid?'

Hasty smiled. 'Just turning up at the right time like you did is enough.'

# EIGHTEEN

'I got some apologies to make,' Sheriff Murray said.

It was a couple of days later, the dust had settled on the action and Hasty and his wife were in their room in the Mexican quarter when a sheepish-looking lawman had come calling.

'The Justice Department in Prescott have gone through their files,' the lawman began, all signs of his former belligerence absent. 'Apparently, before Sheriff Syson died he'd passed them a message to say that he was following up some matter that could tie in with cross-border cases they were following. But he couldn't give a name until he'd investigated further. Then, when his untimely death didn't look suspicious, or seem associated with whatever case he was following, they didn't follow up the matter and closed the file. It's clear now his probings were leading him to Thacker.'

He lowered his voice in summary: 'Fact was, Syson

was a good lawman but, as we both know, he had failings.'

Hasty nodded. 'Figure none of us are black or white.'

The sheriff looked even more sheepish. 'I've misjudged you, Mr Jones. I know I can't make up for that, but I been talking to my missus. Now our boys have growed and left, we got a couple of spare rooms. Ain't the biggest of places, but you're welcome to use 'em till you've sorted things out. And my missus is no mean cook.'

'That's very kind, Sheriff.' The Texan thought on it and added, 'What about my pal Eight-Ball?'

'I'm sure we can find someone to put him up too, free of charge. There's a fair feeling of guilt in the town about the way you been treated. Nothing ain't gonna be too much trouble.'

He looked at Hasty's gun. 'By the way, you want a job, I got a vacancy for deputy. One of Thacker's men came clean in the hope of getting some leniency and told how my deputy Drew had been feeding Thacker with information. The young sidewinder has vamoosed, but I've put out a wire and he should be picked up. The point is, you've shown you got persistence and can handle yourself when things come to the crunch. The job's yours if you want it.'

Hasty shook his head. 'Thanks, Sheriff, but no. Whatever I do, I don't want any more violence. I'm a farm boy at heart.'

At the door the sheriff turned and winked.

'Anyways, Mr Jones, I should have some more good news for you tomorrow.'

He did. Face beaming, he strode in the next day just before lunch. 'Now Thacker's dead, there's all manner of folk coming out of the woodwork prepared to testify that you didn't kill Sheriff Syson.'

Hasty nodded. 'About time.'

'And,' the sheriff went on, 'I've been having a word with the town council. They've offered to pay for the best attorney in town to take up your case for as long as it takes and they've already given him instructions. At the time I gave him as much as I know of your story and he says on the face of it there's a clear case for compensation from the Territory for wrongful imprisonment. At this stage he can't say how long it will take or how much the final figure will be. But you've got an appointment this afternoon to start providing him with chapter and verse.'

And the day's good news didn't end there. On his return from the attorney's office there was a man waiting for him.

The face was familiar. 'Jim Matthews,' Hasty said when recognition hit him. 'Jeez, you've grown. When I worked for your pa out at the Triple C, you weren't even shaving.'

The man rubbed his hand over his stubbly chin and grinned. 'Good to see you, Hasty.'

153

'What can I do for you?' Hasty said after they had shaken hands.

'More the other way round. You being away for a spell, you might not have heard how Thacker got his hands on the Cruz.'

'Heard some account.'

'Well, me and my brothers was aiming to split it when it fell to us on Pa's passing. You remember us – always arguing when we was kids – we couldn't see how we would be happy working the place together. Well, Pa wanted it keeping together so by the terms of the will the place got sold. That way it went to Thacker while we received the proceeds.'

'Yeah, I heard that.'

'At the time, the tale was Thacker had got the original money through shrewd land speculation. And that seemed to be the end of it. But now Thacker's been exposed and an investigation is under way, it seems that was only partly true. Apparently Thacker was already up to his villainous tricks before the purchase. Well, there's a law on the Territorial statute-book stating that any land transaction undertaken with illegal gains is null and void and the land can be confiscated by the Justice Department for disposal at its discretion. What they've decided in this matter is that, provided we give them whatever we have left, even if it's just a token payment, the whole shebang reverts back to us. We reckon we were foolish youngsters and that we should follow Pa's wishes. So we're going to act grown-up and run it together as a joint unit.'

Hasty nodded. 'Your pa would have liked that.'

'Well, none of this would have been possible if you hadn't got Thacker out of the way, so we're in your debt. We were wondering how to handle our obligation when we heard about your place getting burnt up.'

He moved to the door and gestured for Hasty and Charley to follow him. Out on main street he extended an arm and swept it across the horizon visible between the false fronts and adobes. 'So, you go out there with your missus and pick what you want, some place to get started again. The new Triple C will foot the bill – and provide whatever cash you need to get yourselves going.'

Hasty felt a lump coming to his throat. The way he had been treated for three years, the appalling prison conditions, the cold-shouldering he had got from townsfolk on his return, he had begun to hate the world and most of the people in it. But the last couple of days had shown there was goodness in people's hearts. And now. . . .

He pulled Charley to him. 'You know, honey, Arizona ain't so bad after all.' She nestled against his chest and for a moment they watched the fire of the late sun scythe through the clouds. They savoured the moment, with no need to speak.

They remained like that until the silence was broken by a voice. 'Say, boss, I figure you're gonna need a hand in setting up this new outfit of yours.' It was Eight-Ball. 'Think you'll have a place in the scheme of things for an old pardner?'

'Sure.'

'That is,' Eight-Ball added, 'as long as you ain't aiming to grow oranges.'

Hasty grinned. 'Hey, that's an idea. I hadn't thought of that. I hear there's a hell of a profit in oranges these days.'

He put his free hand around his diminutive pal's shoulder, pulling him close to his other side and chuckled. 'Ain't there a drawback to everything?'